Abby told herse... about Greg Has... medical colleagu...

Just because his hair looked as if she should brush it back from his forehead was no reason for her fingers to tingle with yearning. Just because his dark eyes gleamed when they glanced at her was no reason to want to have him stay when she really wanted him gone. Just because his lower lip was slightly fuller than his top lip was no reason for her own to tremble and yearn to feel that sensuous mouth move against her own.

When he looked at her, she blinked. She saw his sister looking at her expectantly. Had Greg said something Abby missed? Had she been caught examining him? Catching herself in the spell of his presence, she tried to ignore the sensations flooding her body.

He radiated sex appeal.

For the first time in her life Abby felt flushed with femininity; she felt sexy—almost alluring.

Dear Reader,

What if…? These two little words serve as the springboard for each romance novel that bestselling author Joan Elliott Pickart writes. "I always go back to that age-old question. My ideas come straight from imagination," she says. And with more than thirty Silhouette novels to her credit, the depth of Joan's imagination seems bottomless! Joan started by taking a class to learn how to write a romance and "felt that this was where I belonged," she recalls. This month Joan delivers *Her Little Secret,* the next from THE BABY BET, where you'll discover what if…a sheriff and a lovely nursery owner decide to foil town matchmakers and "act" like lovers.…

And don't miss the other compelling "what ifs" in this month's Silhouette Special Edition lineup. What if a U.S. Marshal knee-deep in his father's murder investigation discovers his former love is expecting his child? Read *Seven Months and Counting…* by Myrna Temte, the next installment in the STOCKWELLS OF TEXAS series. What if an army ranger, who believes dangerous missions are no place for a woman, learns the only person who can help rescue his sister is a female? Lindsay McKenna brings you this exciting story in *Man with a Mission,* the next book in her MORGAN'S MERCENARIES: MAVERICK HEARTS series. What happens if a dutiful daughter falls in love with the one man her family forbids? Look for Christine Flynn's *Forbidden Love.* What if a single dad falls for a pampered beauty who is not at all accustomed to small-town happily-ever-after? Find out in Nora Roberts's *Considering Kate,* the next in THE STANISLASKIS. And what if the girl-next-door transforms herself to get a man's attention—but is noticed by someone else? Make sure to pick up Barbara McMahon's *Starting with a Kiss.*

What if… Two words with endless possibilities. If you've got your own "what if" scenario, start writing. Silhouette Special Edition would love to read about it.

Happy reading!

Karen Taylor Richman,
Senior Editor

Please address questions and book requests to:
Silhouette Reader Service
U.S.: 3010 Walden Ave., P.O. Box 1325, Buffalo, NY 14269
Canadian: P.O. Box 609, Fort Erie, Ont. L2A 5X3

Starting with a Kiss

BARBARA McMAHON

Silhouette®

SPECIAL EDITION™

Published by Silhouette Books

America's Publisher of Contemporary Romance

To my Dad—for making so many times special
and for always being there for me. I love you!

SILHOUETTE BOOKS

ISBN 0-373-24380-4

STARTING WITH A KISS

Copyright © 2001 by Barbara McMahon

Visit Silhouette at www.eHarlequin.com

Printed in U.S.A.

Books by Barbara McMahon

Silhouette Special Edition

Yours for Ninety Days #1282
Bachelor's Baby Promise #1351
Starting with a Kiss #1380

Silhouette Desire

One Stubborn Cowboy #915
Cowboy's Bride #977
Bride of a Thousand Days #1017
Boss Lady and the Hired Hand #1072
Santa Cowboy #1116
*Cinderella Twin #1154
*The Older Man #1161
The Cowboy and the Virgin #1215

Silhouette Romance

Sheik Daddy #1132
The Sheik's Solution #1422

*Identical Twins!

─────────────────────────────

BARBARA McMAHON

has made California her home since she graduated from
the University of California (Berkely) way back when!
She's convinced she now has the perfect life, living on
the western slopes of the Sierra Nevada Mountains,
sipping lattes on her front porch while she watches the
deer graze nearby, and playing "what if" with different
story ideas. Even though she has sold over three dozen
books, she says she still has another hundred tales to
tell. Barbara also writes for Harlequin Romance.
Readers can write to Barbara at P.O. Box 977, Pioneer,
CA 95666-0777.

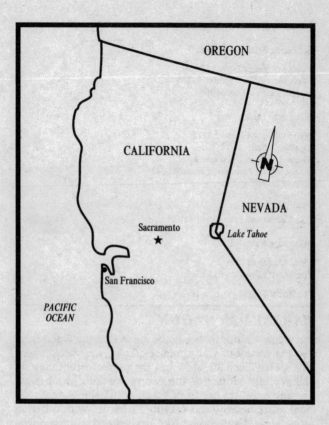

Chapter One

"This is going to be a total disaster!" Abigail Trent exclaimed, frowning at her reflection in the mirror, nerves churning. Taking a deep, slow breath, she tried to calm her jitters.

"Hey, you're the one who said you wanted to make Jeb jealous," her friend Kim said, aiming the hair spray at the back of Abby's head. The hiss of the spray sounded before Abby replied. She held her breath as she was enveloped in the mist. She couldn't deny Kim's remark. When she'd first learned Jeb Stuart had stopped calling because he was seeing someone else, she'd been hurt, and furious. She'd thought they'd be heading for the altar one day. Instead, he was totally involved with someone else.

Stepping away from the mirror, she shook her head. "Do you think it'll work? Even though I don't look a bit like myself in this getup, I'm not sure it's going to be enough. I wish I was a fabulous blonde with a figure to die for." She frowned again. "What has me worried about tonight is I have no business accepting the donation. I'm not sure I should even be going to this presentation banquet. The hospital's chief administrator should accept. Or the head of Internal Medicine, not some newly appointed doctor of pediatrics."

"Carol's family specifically asked for you," Kim said gently.

Abby nodded, her eyes filling with tears. She missed her friend so much! It wasn't fair. She'd died so young! Too young! She'd had her entire life ahead of her, until a drunk driver had ended it by ramming into her car.

"Don't do that or all your makeup will run and we'll have to start over," Kim fussed, touching her shoulder in sympathy.

Abby looked up at the ceiling, blinking rapidly. "No time for that! Dr. Hastings will be here any second. And the last thing I plan to do is keep him waiting!"

Kim began to tidy all the bottles and containers she'd brought. "I can't believe you've worked at the same hospital for six months and you still call him Dr. Hastings. Don't you have any kind of informality there?"

"Not with him," Abby said, stepping in front of the mirror again. The push-up bra gave her cleavage she'd never expected, and the painted-on dress displayed it for all the world to see. She tried to pull the dress up to a more modest level. Kim slapped her hand.

"Stop that. It's fine."

"I feel I've been poured into this thing. I'm not sure

this was a good idea after all.'' All her doubts and insecurities rose up to mock her.

''Hey, you wanted Jeb to see you in a different light. This is it. No scrubs, no lab coat, no jeans. Just pure Abby.''

''This does not look pure!''

Kim laughed. ''Okay, then mysterious, sultry, sexy Abby. Jeb will eat his heart out.''

''I wish.'' Sighing softly, Abby turned when the doorbell sounded. ''Great, nemesis himself.''

''Why did you agree to go with Dr. Hastings if you don't like him?''

''Politics, why else? When the chief of staff heard I didn't have an escort, he insisted Dr. Hastings take me tonight. Who am I to argue with the head man? Being low on the totem pole, I need all the friends in high places I can get.''

She hurried from the bedroom when the second peal came. The high heels felt strange, the turquoise dress was definitely two sizes too small, and her teased and tousled hair wouldn't move in a tornado, it had so much spray holding it. She wished she was spending the evening at home in comfy sweats.

Why had she ever concocted the idea of trying to compete with Jeb's new love?

Taking another deep breath, she threw open the door, bracing herself for the onslaught of feelings she always experienced when she faced Greg Hastings. It didn't seem to get easier, though she'd known him for six months.

She'd been in staff meetings with him. Seen him in the corridors dozens of times since she'd started working at Merrimac General Hospital—usually in the company of some nurse gushing in adoration. Not that it was hard to see what they found attractive.

Everything.

From his height, to the breadth of his shoulders, to the high cheekbones and dark, all-knowing eyes. Tanned as if he spent time outdoors and didn't care about sunscreen, he always looked healthy and vital.

Tonight he looked perfect in the charcoal-gray suit, white shirt and deep maroon tie. But he looked equally wonderful when she'd seen him in the white lab coat he wore attending staff meetings, or even the rumpled scrubs after a day in surgery.

"Hi," she said, trying to ignore the fluttering in her stomach that had suddenly grown worse. "I'll just be a sec. Want to come in?" She turned, without waiting for an answer, and snatched up her evening purse and the coat she knew she'd need for San Francisco's cool evenings.

Kim came out from the bedroom, her tote on her shoulder. "Have fun," she said. Her eyes widened with interest when she spotted Greg Hastings.

He'd stepped inside and stood studying Abby's apartment, or what he could see of it. Abby could imagine his disdain for her feminine furnishings. Not that she cared. She had more immediate things to worry about—like getting through tonight's presentation. She could do it. Take the check that would be given by the Walker family's attorney. Give her brief acceptance speech on behalf of the hospital. She could do that for her friend's sake. She had to.

When Kim cleared her throat, Abby rushed into introductions.

"Kim, this is Dr. Hastings." Abby motioned to Kim and said, "My neighbor, Kim Saunders."

"Hello, Dr. Hastings, I'm pleased to meet you," Kim said with a wide smile. She made it a point to cross the room and shake his hand.

Abby envied her friend's walk. If she practiced for years, she'd never get that sexy sway. Was that what men wanted?

"Kim, a pleasure, and it's Greg." His deep voice seemed genuinely pleased to meet her. Abby looked at him, and wished he sounded half as pleased to see her when they met at the hospital.

"You take good care of Abby tonight, Greg," she said flirtatiously.

"I'm ready," Abby said, wishing she had her friend's ease around men. But just being around Greg Hastings tied her tongue in knots and made her stomach feel as if a dozen butterflies were playing rugby.

Greg turned to her, letting his gaze run down the length of her. The slight amusement in his eyes flustered her even more. Was something wrong? Had Kim missed something?

Tilting his head to one side, he commented, "You look different from the way I'm used to seeing you at the hospital."

"I couldn't very well wear a lab coat," she said shortly. But his look only increased her uncertainty about the appropriateness of her dress. Of her whole appearance. After years of concentrating on study and work, she felt like a novice in the social scene. Time to make changes. Starting tonight!

Raising her chin, she glared at him.

His lips twitched as if in amusement. "My car is downstairs." Without another word, he stood aside for her to precede him out the door. Kim slipped through and waved.

"Tell me all about it tomorrow," she called to Abby as she headed down the hall to her apartment.

In only moments Abby was seated in the luxurious interior of Greg Hastings's silver Mercedes. He pulled away from the curb with ease and headed toward the downtown restaurant where the banquet was being held.

Feeling awkward in the silence, Abby reviewed what she planned to say when the endowment check was presented. Her heart ached. Carol Walker had been her best friend—she and Jeb. Both Abby's age, just thirty, they had gone through four years of college together, medical school, then done their internships in hospitals close enough to hang out or study together when they weren't working. She and Carol and Jeb— the three musketeers, they'd been dubbed early on. The best of friends.

Now one was dead—and the other just as gone.

Aware the silence had lasted a long time, Abby looked at her companion.

"Thanks for the ride," she said.

He shrugged. "I was going anyway."

"I can find my own way home. You needn't bother."

He flicked her a glance. "I'll take you home."

He could sound a bit more friendly, she thought. The embarrassment she'd felt when the chief of staff had informed her Dr. Hastings would pick her up hadn't totally faded. If she had thought about it early enough, she could have found someone to escort her tonight, couldn't she?

But Jeb was the one she would have chosen, and he was too entangled with Sara, the blond bombshell.

"Tell me about Carol Walker," Greg said, "and

why her family is providing this endowment for the hospital.''

''She had just been hired at the hospital when she was killed,'' Abby said slowly. The now-familiar ache in her heart seemed to spread. ''She was so excited about being a doctor. Thrilled to be taken on at Merrimac General. I guess we all are when we start out.'' She looked at him, wondering if she'd become as cynical as he after she'd been working a few years. She hoped not!

''You don't have to say anything, I know what you're thinking,'' she said defensively.

''And that is?''

''That we all seem young and idealistic and it won't last. But I'm still excited and not afraid to admit it! Carol had her whole life ahead of her—finally able to start the career she'd spent years training for. She had just gotten engaged and was making plans to get married, have kids.'' Abby's voice broke and she looked away, furious with herself for letting this man see her emotions.

''Tough break.''

''It's unfair.''

''Life often is.''

''Spoken like a true cynic.''

''Is that how you see me—cynical?''

''Aren't you? Your views stated in the staff meetings sure seem to point that way. I don't want to become like you.''

''Then let's hope you can stay in your cozy cocoon.''

''I'm not encased in a cocoon. I've been working as a doctor for some time now. I love it. It has its bad moments, of course—when, no matter what, I can't help someone. But mostly, it's just what I always wanted.''

He slid the car to a stop in front of the restaurant. Abby slipped out when the doorman held the door open, wishing the dress hadn't ridden up so much. She tugged it in place, pulling it up a bit for good measure.

Good manners dictated she wait for Greg, but she wished she could just go into the banquet room alone. The reality was she'd be spending the entire evening with him. She glanced down at her wrist. No watch— darn. How long would it be before the banquet ended and he took her home?

She regretted her outburst. She and Greg Hastings didn't see eye to eye, but there was no call to start an awkward evening off with hostility. Not that she was going to apologize. There was nothing wrong in expressing her thoughts. He was cynical. Even he hadn't denied it.

The banquet room was almost full when they entered. Walking toward the designated head table, Abby nodded to two or three acquaintances and quickly scanned the room to see if Jeb had come. He'd been invited—as a close friend of Carol's. Her family was not coming. It was still too soon after her death.

She saw him seated at a table to the right. Immediately her gaze was drawn to the blond beauty at his side. There was no denying Sara was gorgeous. Frowning, Abby marched onward, feeling self-conscious with the drastic change in her appearance. And with the looks she was getting from people who knew her at the hospital.

She took another deep breath. This technique for calming jittery nerves seemed highly overrated. Any more deep breaths and she'd hyperventilate. Her nervousness grew as more and more people swung around to stare at her. Was it simple curiosity, or was it the dress?

Maybe, just maybe, she'd gone a tad overboard.

Or were they fascinated by the fact that she had arrived with Greg Hastings? Would it be all over Merrimac General tomorrow that Dr. Abigail Trent couldn't get a date, that she had to be set up?

How long had it been since she'd been on a date? A real honest-to-goodness date—not a night out with Jeb and Carol? She shied away from thinking about all the evenings the three of them had shared. She would not let her emotions choke her again.

Tilting her chin, she stepped up to the head table, grateful to be able to sit. At least she didn't feel so much on display.

Unfortunately, Greg Hastings sat right beside her. Too close, actually. She peeked at him through her lashes, then looked quickly away. Could she pretend her beeper had sounded and dash away? No. She owed it to Carol's memory to accept the endowment.

She recognized some of the administrative staff, doctors, two head nurses. Glancing around, she looked for the Walkers' attorney.

The subtle scent of Greg's aftershave wafted her way, starting a curious reaction. Her heart rate sped up, her senses became more alert. A strange bud of interest curled deep inside. Swallowing hard, she tried to ignore the sensations, tried to ignore how awkward she felt. It was just a meal, a business commitment.

''What a large crowd,'' she murmured, wishing desperately she had the gift of small talk. Maybe she could pretend he was a patient and talk to him like a doctor.

That wouldn't work. Almost all her patients were

under ten, and Greg Hastings was nothing like a ten-
year-old! She even wondered if he'd ever been ten.
She had trouble envisioning him as anything other
than the successful surgeon he was.

A laugh almost escaped as she imagined him as a
dedicated surgeon when only ten. She glanced at him
and found his dark eyes on her. Her breath caught—
that gaze felt as dangerous as skydiving. Her breath-
lessness couldn't be any worse if she'd jumped out of
a plane!

He reached for his water glass and her gaze was
drawn to his hands. As a skilled surgeon, did he take
them for granted? His palms were large, as fitted a
man his size, his fingers long.

What would they feel like holding hers? They had
never touched, had no reason to. But for a moment
she wondered what it would feel like to have her hand
engulfed in his.

She raised her eyes and Greg quirked up one eyebrow, as if in silent inquiry. Heat flooded her face.
She was no better than those silly nurses who fawned
all over him.

Ben Taylor, chief of staff for Merrimac General,
joined them at the table. Greg stood and shook the
older man's hand, smiling in warm welcome.

In his right cheek a dimple appeared. Abby's heart
skipped a beat. She used to daydream about some
dashing knight sweeping her off her feet—and in her
mind he'd always been a rugged rogue—with dimples.

Where did women get these silly notions? Greg was
a respected member of the hospital staff, a surgeon
with a growing reputation. Not some man to have fantasy dreams about. They were colleagues. Nothing
more. A colleague, moreover, she wasn't sure she even

liked. And if his attitude toward her was anything to go by, the feeling was mutual!

Seated beside him, she could almost feel the power and assurance that cloaked him. She definitely felt a tingling awareness that had nothing to do with business, but was totally personal.

It was simply sex appeal. Oh, Lord, did he have that in spades!

She looked around and caught the eye of one of the doctors from the emergency room. His knowing smirk startled her. What—? When his gaze moved to Greg, the oddest thought struck. Did he think she and Dr. Hastings were *dating?* How ludicrous. As if Greg Hastings, heartthrob of Merrimac General, would ever consider dating someone like her!

"We'll wait until the dessert is served before starting the speeches," Ben remarked.

She nodded and involuntarily glanced at Jeb's table to study the vivacious woman at his side. That was the kind of woman men liked—beautiful and gifted with the ability to make small talk.

"Is there someone you want to speak with? There's time before they start serving dinner," Greg said softly as he sat down when Ben moved on to speak to another staff member at the next table.

She met his eyes. "What do you mean?"

"You keep staring at that table. If there's someone you want to talk with, you have time."

"No, there's no one." She looked away. He was too perceptive. She'd better make sure she didn't look at Jeb's table again anytime soon.

Greg studied her for a moment, perplexed with the enigma that was Abigail Trent. He'd been surprised yesterday when Ben had asked him if he would escort Dr. Trent to tonight's banquet. Used to the ploys of women on the make, he'd instinctively suspected an ulterior motive in the request.

When she'd opened her door tonight, he'd been shocked to see the change from quiet, slightly prickly young Dr. Trent to—to what? He didn't mind women dressing up for a date, but there was something too much about the way she was dressed tonight. Not that he'd ever mention it. He had two sisters and knew better than to make any negative comment when a woman had taken pains to dress to the nines.

And it wasn't that he didn't appreciate the way the dress showed off her figure. Who would have suspected behind those ubiquitous lab coats Dr. Abigail Trent had a tempting femininity that could capture a man's interest in less than five seconds.

Tempting?

Greg watched her take another deep breath. Did she have any idea what doing that did to the dress?

While her attire suggested one thing, her attitude puzzled him. Had she dolled herself up to make a play for him? If so, she'd lost her nerve. So far he felt more like a fifth wheel than the center of her attraction.

Wryly looking away, Greg wondered if he was starting to believe the hype his secretary told him every day. He did not expect every woman he met to fall for him. He didn't want anyone to, if the truth be known. He'd been down that road once—and had no intention of ever going again.

But neither was he used to taking a woman out and having her attention focused three tables away!

He frowned at the thought. He didn't care. He was

merely doing his duty as a favor to the chief of staff. When tonight's event ended, they'd go back to normal. He'd see her a couple of times a month at staff meetings, maybe pass in the hallway. Or consult if she had a patient who needed surgery. That would be the extent of their involvement.

By the time dinner had ended, his companion was definitely displaying signs of nervousness. Amusement began to sweep through him as he studied her, taking in her agitated air, her held breath. She was a doctor, held the power of life and death in her hands, and she was nervous about accepting a check on behalf of the hospital? He hadn't felt that anxious when he'd diagnosed his very first patient.

Interested in how she'd handle herself, Greg sat back to watch, still trying to figure the woman out. And he glanced to the table she had under observation, trying to figure out which man sitting there was the one she was interested in.

By the time the evening ended, Greg felt almost sorry for Abigail Trent. She'd given a good speech when accepting the endowment. Her voice had broken once, but that had added to the poignancy of the evening. Several colleagues spoke warmly about Carol Walker, about the lost potential, the tragic accident that had claimed her life. The speeches seemed to upset Abigail.

He could tell the entire evening was proving a strain and almost felt her relief when they rose to leave. The next time Ben Taylor asked him for a favor, he'd be sure he had other plans.

A young man from the table she'd been staring at

came up to her. Greg suddenly felt Abigail's tension increase.

"Abby, I nearly didn't recognize you. What did you do to yourself?" he asked bluntly, frowning as he looked her over from head to toe.

"Hi, Jeb." She smiled at him almost in relief. "I don't always wear lab coats, you know."

From the bright smile and the way she looked up at the young man, Greg suspected he'd been her focus of interest all evening.

"I guess not, but neither do you wear dresses like this." His gaze held obvious disapproval. "You look like a tart."

Hot color instantly stained Abby's checks.

A feeling of protectiveness suddenly and unexpectedly surged through Greg. She might not be dressed as conservatively as she normally did, but there was no reason to insult her! He stepped closer.

"I don't believe we've been introduced. I'm Greg Hastings." He held out his hand, coming between Abigail and the rude young man as if he could cut the tension by his presence.

"Jeb Stuart. I'm an old friend of Abby's. And Carol's." Jeb held out his hand.

Greg resisted the temptation to annihilate him with a punishing handshake. It was surprisingly hard. He thought that kind of behavior ended in high school. Obviously not.

"We have to be going," he said to Abby, offering an out.

She took it gratefully. "Yes, of course. Bye, Jeb."

As they wound their way through the crowd, Greg kept an eye on Abby. Her head held high, she refused to meet anyone's eye, but walked determinedly toward the door. The deep pink in her cheeks made her blue eyes sparkle. He'd seen that same kind of sparkle once or twice when she became impassioned about a topic in the staff meeting.

He admired her for holding up after Jeb's insult.

There seemed to be more to Dr. Trent than he'd first thought, even though none of it concerned him. She'd made that abundantly clear during the evening.

Nevertheless, his interest was piqued—he wanted to know about the relationship between her and Jeb Stuart. Were they lovers who had had a falling-out? He frowned, not liking the idea at all.

They had to wait for the parking attendant to bring his car. The air blew briskly down the canyon between buildings, the cool ocean fog already blanketing the city. Abby huddled in her coat, buttoned to the neck, her gaze on her toes.

"You did well in your speech," he said to break the silence.

"Thanks."

Another couple from the banquet left, calling goodnights.

Just then a taxi came to a stop in front of the restaurant. Before he could react, Greg watched Abby dart into the cab. Halting before closing the door, she offered a phony polite smile.

"Thanks for being my escort, Dr. Hastings. I'll see myself home."

So much for thinking the lady had a hidden agenda, Greg thought wryly as he watched the cab pull away. Two seconds later his car arrived.

"Timing is everything," he murmured, giving the attendant a tip and sliding in behind the wheel. For a moment he considered following Abby to make sure she got home safely, then discarded the idea. The woman had made her choice clear. But he couldn't help wondering what her thinking had been—before and after seeing Jeb Stuart.

Who was the real Abigail Trent—quiet, shy doctor? Or budding femme fatale?

Chapter Two

"Rats!" Abby murmured as she rushed down the hospital corridor. She wanted to run, but that was very definitely frowned upon at the hospital unless there was a life-threatening emergency. She was late— again. Which didn't threaten anyone—except herself. The last staff meeting she'd been late for, Dr. Taylor had dripped sarcasm, and she'd had to endure the laughter of the whole staff.

Sometimes it couldn't be helped. They were all doctors, they should understand that!

She turned the corner and slowed down a tad to get her breathing under control. Being late wasn't the only reason she dreaded this meeting. Everyone in attendance would have been at the banquet last week. Everyone would know she'd made a fool of herself trying to compete in an area she had no business even venturing! She was a doctor, and a darn good one.

Forget Jeb and concentrate on her work, she told herself for the millionth time.

True to her worst expectations, every eye immediately swung her way when she opened the conference room door and stepped inside. The lone empty seat was at the far end of the room. Murmuring an apology to Dr. Taylor, she began to walk toward it, only realizing at the last moment it was right next to Greg Hastings. Could life get any worse?

"Nice of you to join us, Dr. Trent," Dr. Taylor said.

Excuses didn't help. She nodded and sat, wishing she'd just skipped the meeting. She could have found out the news later from one of her friends. Susan Shattner looked at her and smiled, rolling her eyes. Susan had been late once, as Abby recalled. She too had been subject to Dr. Taylor's scathing comments.

But never Dr. Hastings. Of course not, wasn't he perfect?

Concentrating on Dr. Taylor, she did her best to ignore the man beside her. At least the chief of staff didn't stop to make a snide comment this time.

"...which leads to the next item on the agenda. As you know, Steve Johnston co-chaired the conference committee with Greg. Due to the death of his father and the needs his mother continues to have, he's leaving at the end of the month to return to Baltimore. I've relieved him of his conference responsibilities. But—" Dr. Taylor looked around the table, his gaze settling on Abby, "we still need a co-chair for the committee. Most of the work is done, but there will still be decisions to make, and continued supervision to make sure it comes off flawlessly. I'm appointing Abigail Trent to the position."

Abby stared at him, dumbfounded. Incredulously

she swung around to Greg Hastings. She was to share the committee chair position with him? The man who had witnessed her most embarrassing night ever? She couldn't do it, not in a million years!

His cool gaze met hers, as if challenging her to say something.

She looked at Dr. Taylor again. "I don't think I'm right for this," she said. "I don't have enough experience."

"I'm not asking you to present a workshop, just assist Greg in coordinating the event. Sally Chapel and Bob Montgomery are also on the committee, to help as needed. But the final decisions will rest with you and Greg." The subject was closed as far as he was concerned. He picked up a sheet of paper.

"Next up, the scheduling changes the Nursing Administration is requesting. It impacts primarily..."

Abby's mind went blank. She couldn't believe the assignment. Of all the people to be paired with. Not only did she and Dr. Hastings scarcely speak to each other, he'd been right there last week when Jeb had been so scathing. At least she'd been spared others hearing Jeb's insult. Her cheeks burned again just remembering. She wished she could forget every moment, but her memory was excellent.

As, she was sure, was Dr. Hastings's.

He slid a note in front of her: "My office after?"

Idly she noticed his bold handwriting, the easy-to-read note reminding her of his reputation for saying what he meant and never mind whose toes he stepped on—no emotions, no wasted energy.

She frowned and picked up her pen, scrawling back: "Can't, I have appointments."

Two minutes later the paper was returned: "When, then?"

She had a vague idea of cornering Dr. Taylor after the meeting and arguing against the assignment, but upon reflection, that might appear less than professional. And she could use the experience—if only it wasn't with Dr. Hastings!

She dashed off the numeral four and slid the paper to her left. Her attention on the exchange of notes, she'd lost the trend of the discussion.

When the chief of staff called on Greg for an update on the conference, Abby tried her best to focus on what he was saying. After all, she'd have to come up to speed quickly.

But she found herself studying his hands as he held his papers, listening to the intonation and cadence of his voice as his richly masculine tones filled the room, cool and self-assured. He always was in control. Too controlled? she wondered. Did he ever let go? Maybe with close friends.

A close woman friend?

Frowning, she jerked her thoughts back to the presentation. She wasn't going down *that* road. Whatever Greg Hastings did in his spare time was his business, not hers!

"Which brings us up to the ball on Saturday the twentieth. We have several civic organizations pledging support, so we should realize the goal we set." Greg slanted a glance at Abby. "My new co-chair and I can check out the ballroom this week and make sure everything is on track. I trust Steve's judgment, but this was one area I've neglected. With him gone, I'll bring us both up to speed on that aspect."

The ball! A major fund-raiser for the hospital, the

annual charity event drew corporate sponsors and individuals alike. Held at the St. Francis Hotel in San Francisco, it was lavish and elegant. Or so she'd heard. It would be the first one she had attended.

Abby looked warily at the chief of staff. That was one event she'd make sure she had a date for even if she had to hire somebody off the street!

"Good job, Greg. Any other items we need to address?" Dr. Taylor asked the staff.

Not hearing any, the meeting was adjourned.

"Susan, can I speak with you?" Abby jumped up before she could be cornered by Greg Hastings and, gathering her notes, hastened to join her friend.

"So," Susan said, glancing over her shoulder. "You and Greg. Is this a trend? You two went to that banquet last week, now co-chairs? Hmm, anything you want to share with a friend?"

"Yes, I wish I didn't have this assignment. And didn't you hear, last week was a duty escort arranged by Dr. Taylor."

"Not according to the rampant rumors going around. Apparently there's a nurse on the surgical wing who is very miffed."

"Oh, for heaven's sake. Doesn't anyone have anything better to do than gossip?"

"About our sexy Dr. Hastings? I doubt it."

"Oh, well, if it's just about him—"

"Not exactly."

Abby waited until the hallway was almost deserted, then dared to ask, "Not exactly?"

"There was some speculation as to the way you were dressed."

Abby groaned with embarrassment. "I knew it, it was too much, wasn't it."

"Certainly not your style," her friend said gently.

"My neighbor helped. She's a bit more flamboyant than I am."

"I thought you looked fantastic."

"Well, some parties thought I looked like a tart."

"Greg?"

She shrugged. "If he did, he was polite enough to refrain from saying so."

"Who?"

"Just a friend who obviously felt no such restraints."

"And the purpose of that dress?"

Abby glanced around to make sure they couldn't be overheard. "I was trying to make someone take notice."

"Honey, I think the entire male population of the hospital took notice. Super doctor by day, femme fatale by night!"

Abby scowled. "Not my intent."

Susan studied her for a moment. "There's a happy medium—you just need some pointers."

"Are you volunteering?" Abby asked, diverted temporarily by the idea. She had been over the top last week. And it hadn't done a speck of good. Jeb had not found her attractive—just the opposite.

"No, but I know someone who would be perfect." The teasing look in her eyes made Abby wary.

"Right—in my spare time. But in the meantime, I didn't stop you to discuss my social life. I wanted to ask you about that procedure you were talking about a few weeks ago. I have a kid who is not responding to normal treatment."

Thankfully, their conversation turned to medicine

and Abby was able to put aside the memory of that embarrassing night.

Until she showed up at Dr. Hastings's office that afternoon just prior to four. She made sure she was not late. His door was ajar, the secretary's desk empty.

Should she wait, or just go in? Taking a step closer, she heard voices. Someone was in with Greg. She'd wait.

"Shall I leave the door open when your four-o'clock appointment arrives?" The voice came from Greg's secretary, Rose. Abby had met her once before.

"Why?" The sound of papers being shuffled drifted outside the door.

"Your reputation, of course," Rose said with asperity. "After the way Dr. Trent was dressed when you took her to the banquet, you have to know she's trying to vamp you."

"Vamp me? Where do you come up with these terms, Rose?"

Abby's cheeks began to burn again. Did the entire hospital think she had been trying to make a play for Dr. Hastings?

"I'm into retro. Anyway, I'm looking out for you."

"Yeah, the man most likely to sweep a woman off her feet."

"One look at your killer smile and every woman in sight will swoon."

He laughed.

Abby stepped closer, charmed by the rich tone of Greg's laughter. If only she didn't feel she was the butt of the joke. Damn, why had she let Kim talk her into all that makeup and that dress?

"Rose, you're priceless. When Dr. Trent arrives, show her in, and then shut the door."

"What was that about last week?"

"Darn if I know. I expected a quiet, mousy physician to open her door, so I was as surprised as anyone else at the way she looked."

There were several seconds of silence. Mousy? Was that how he saw her? Did everyone see her that way? Abby turned to tiptoe away when Rose spoke again, her voice pensive.

"You know, maybe she's looking to change her image. You could help."

"Me?" Greg laughed again. "I don't think so, Rose."

"Think about it, Pam could get her some clothes that suited her personality. Elise could give her pointers on walking and looking sexy, and how to apply makeup for an understated look. I'm serious, Greg."

"I will not think about it. Thanks for the suggestions, Rose, but Dr. Trent is well able to look after herself."

"Hmm, I wonder."

Abby spun around and headed for the hall. She'd rather be thought tardy than be caught eavesdropping—especially when she'd been the topic under discussion. Heat scorched her cheeks. She wanted to dash away and never face the man again. Or his cheeky secretary.

She reached the water fountain and stopped for a drink, hoping the color that had flooded her cheeks would fade. This was worse than she'd expected. She thought she and Greg would just briefly touch base. He'd hand her a file of the committee information and she could escape. Now she'd be wondering what he was thinking the entire time.

She cleared her throat as she drew near the secretary's desk. Rose was just coming from Greg's office. Young and stylish, she was well thought of throughout the hospital, fiercely loyal to her boss, and the hospital in general.

"Hi, Dr. Trent. You're right on time," she said, smiling brightly.

Abby nodded, avoiding Rose's eyes. "Is Dr. Hastings ready?"

Greg appeared in the doorway, almost filling the space. Abby swallowed and tried to ignore the familiar fluttering in her stomach. Tried not to dwell on the conversation she'd overheard.

"Since we'll be working closely on the conference, don't you think you should call me Greg?" he said easily, leaning casually against the doorjamb and crossing his arms over his chest as he assessed her.

He'd noticed, had he, that she'd never been able to call him by his first name? Had anyone else noticed?

As she drew closer and he didn't budge, she wondered if he would move to allow her through the door?

He did, at the last second, his eyes dancing in taunting amusement.

She stepped inside his office, her defenses on the ready. She was not some woman to be swept away by his killer smile, or anything else. She was here under protest, and would do only what she had to in order to pull her weight on the committee.

Deliberately Greg shut the door.

"Have a seat." He gestured to one of the visitor chairs then took his seat behind his desk. Seconds later he began to fill her in on all the steps taken in preparation for the conference. Rose was handling many of the details and follow-up work. The schedule had been settled, speakers committed, programs drafted for the printers.

Several minutes later he looked up. "That leaves the ball. Steve was working on that, and I expect you can take over from where he left. The orchestra has been booked, the menu finalized, former donors contacted. There will be only the routine tasks left now. If you could supervise this aspect, it would help. Let me or Rose know if you need anything."

Abby nodded, wondering if she could leave now. She'd make sure she managed everything without ever bothering Greg or his outspoken secretary.

He slid the folder to her. "This pretty much recaps everything."

He leaned back in his chair and studied her. "Will you be needing an escort to the ball?" he asked.

"No," she said, gathering the folder and standing. Was she never going to live that down?

"Just checking. It would be easier to know early rather than the day of the event."

"It wasn't my idea last time. I assure you, I'll find someone to take me to the ball. And if I don't, Dr. Taylor will never learn it from me!"

He looked at her thoughtfully. "You'll find someone? No steady man in your life?"

"Not that it's any business of yours, Dr. Hastings, but no there's not." She clutched the folder to her chest and edged toward the door.

"Greg," he said, standing.

She nodded abruptly. "If that's all, I do have other things to do."

"That's all for now. Review the information and let me know if you have any questions. Are you free tomorrow at two?"

"Tomorrow? Why?"

"So we can check out the ballroom at the hotel. If that time's not good, let Rose know when you can go. I'll drive."

"I don't have my calendar with me, but I expect it won't be convenient. I see patients all day long, you know."

He nodded. "I have a gall bladder first thing tomorrow, but then am free. If you're not, we'll make it later. Say seven?"

Abby wanted to protest, but she didn't have an alternative time that would be convenient. Never seeing him again would be convenient, but wasn't going to happen.

"Fine. Seven, tomorrow." Turning, she almost fled from his office.

Rose looked up in surprise. "Finished already?"

Abby nodded and kept walking. She had more than twenty-four hours to get herself under control before seeing him again. She'd be the epitome of professionalism.

Given time, there'd be other tidbits to capture the attention of the hospital gossips. Her one foray into life on the wild side would fade.

And she'd learned her lesson. She couldn't compete with Sara. Jeb was gone. She had to accept it. And truth to tell, even if overnight she became some beautiful sex symbol, she didn't want a man who would turn away at the first sight of a new face.

What did Greg Hastings look for? she wondered.

When Greg rang Abby's doorbell the next evening, he felt a slight rise of anticipation. So far he couldn't quite call their encounters productive. She always seemed poised to take off at any second—her leaving him in front of the restaurant last week a case in point. Yet he was almost looking forward to their get-together this evening. For a little while, at least, she'd have to give him some attention. Maybe he could better understand the woman.

She opened the door. For a split second he was disappointed she hadn't done her hair up as if she'd just tumbled out of bed. And that she wasn't wearing a dress that displayed every inch of her body like a man's fantasy. She wore the expected tailored suit, her hair pulled back in a low ponytail. And she was not wearing any makeup. From one extreme to another.

"Good evening, I'm ready." She stepped into the hall and pulled the door shut, checking the lock.

"Despite the rumors, I don't believe you are trying to seduce me," he murmured.

"What?" She looked up, startled.

At least that got a reaction. "Seduction needs more privacy than your hall." He turned toward the elevator. "I'll have to reassure Rose that we have a strictly business relationship."

"I don't feel we have any kind of relationship at all, Dr. Hastings." Abby fell into step beside him. "I certainly didn't ask Dr. Taylor to press you into service last week. And I could check out the hotel ballroom on my own this evening. You don't have to accompany me."

"But it's so much easier if we check it out together." Greg said smoothly. "If you don't call me by my name from now on, *Abigail,* I'll have to take drastic measures!"

"Such as?" She punched the down call button for

the elevator with more force than he thought necessary.

"I don't know," he teased, suddenly enjoying himself for the first time in a long while. As the elevator doors slid open, they stepped inside. An older couple already was in the car.

"Maybe kiss you," he said outrageously just to get another rise from her.

She glared at him. Silence reigned.

When the elevator reached the lobby, the older couple gave them a brief glance and stepped out.

Abby watched until they were out the front door before spinning around.

"That was totally uncalled-for. I can just imagine what they were thinking!"

With a gentle nudge, he urged her from the elevator and across the marble floor of the lobby.

"What they're thinking, *Greg*."

"Greg, Greg, Greg! There, are you satisfied?"

Holding the lobby door for her, Greg watched as she stormed out to the sidewalk. For a moment the image of her saying the words in a different context slammed into him.

Abigail Trent and bed? The thought was ludicrous. She had no interest in him and he certainly could afford no long-term interest in any woman.

When they reached the hotel on Union Square, Greg availed himself of valet parking, wondering if Abby planned to dash into another cab when they'd finished.

"For the record, I'm taking you home," he said as they entered the St. Francis Hotel. The old San Francisco landmark was centrally located and perfect for the lavish fund-raising ball.

"There's no need—"

"Actually, there is. I have something to discuss with you," he said as they entered the lobby.

"About the conference?"

"Sort of."

"And you can't discuss it here?" Abby asked suspiciously.

"No."

They met the events coordinator and soon had a tour of the ballroom and the kitchen that would service the event. They discussed decorations and music, in addition to amenities like the cloakroom, anticipated space needed for valet parking, and rooms for guests who would like to avail themselves of the chance to spend the night after the ball.

Greg noticed Abby's questions were well thought out, and seemed to cover all aspects of the event. He knew she had never attended one of the balls, but she honed in on the aspects most likely to cause problems at the last minute.

He wasn't sure why Ben had assigned Abby as co-chair, but she proved she'd do her share.

It was after nine by the time they finished. Greg took her arm in a gentle grip.

"I won't run away," Abby said irritably.

"Indulge me," he said.

"You don't trust me, Doctor?"

"Not any further than I can throw you. But don't take it personally, I don't trust any woman."

"There's a comment that begs for elaboration."

"Not tonight. Here's the car."

The ride to her place was silent. Greg wondered what she was thinking—and how best to broach the subject Rose insisted he bring up.

When he stopped in front of her apartment building, he turned off the engine and turned to look at her.

"It's about the other night."

Warily she looked at him. "What about it?"

He reached into his pocket for a business card and handed it to her. "Rose suggested you might be in the market for some new clothes."

Abby made no move to take the card, looking at it as if it would bite.

"There's nothing wrong with my clothes."

"I never said there was." He was handling it all wrong. On the other hand, he couldn't imagine any way being considered right. Rose should have talked to her. It would have been better coming from another woman.

He dropped the card in her lap. "My sister has a boutique on Maiden Lane. Tell her I sent you and maybe she'll give you a discount. On the other hand, if it's a day she's mad at me, she'll probably charge you extra."

Looking at him suspiciously, Abby gingerly picked up the card. "Why are you doing this?"

Greg shrugged, wondering the same thing himself. As a rule he didn't become involved in other people's personal lives. "To stop Rose from haranguing me every minute. She's a terrific secretary. I'd be lost without her. But she can drive me crazy when she gets some idea in her head. She's convinced there was some hidden message in the way you were dressed the other night."

Abby fingered the card, taking a deep breath and meeting his gaze. "Thank you." Opening the door, she stepped out onto the sidewalk. "I'll think about it."

Chapter Three

Abby watched as Greg's car sped away. What was she, some charity case? Crumpling the card in her hand, she headed inside. Entering her apartment a moment later, she tossed it toward the trash. It fell short.

His carefully crafted words echoed in her mind. At least he hadn't laughed aloud. In fact he'd looked downright uncomfortable.

She almost smiled. Had he really expected her to believe that story about Rose pushing him around? A man less likely to be pushed by anyone she had yet to meet.

Still, it wouldn't hurt to go shopping and just look.

She picked up the card and smoothed it out. Maybe he'd done it out of the genuine goodness of his heart. She laughed at that. From what she'd heard, Dr. Hastings didn't have a heart.

The phone rang.

"Hello?"

"I was also supposed to add my sister would be happy to give you any pointers you might like. Like on your hair or something."

From the background noise, she knew he was on his cell phone. How had he gotten her number?

"Why?"

"The consensus seems to be you are trying to capture some man's attention."

"So much for being subtle," she murmured, sinking down onto the sofa. "Who shares this consensus?" The gossip had been even more widespread than she'd suspected if Greg Hastings was hearing it.

"That's not important. Is it correct?"

"No." Honesty nudged. "Well, sort of, maybe."

"I hope you don't give diagnoses that way."

"No, I don't. And this conversation is over."

She hung up. If she could turn back the clock, she'd never have agreed to Kim's outlandish suggestion. But of course if she could turn back the clock, she'd make sure Carol never got into a car that fateful day.

When the phone rang again, she snatched it up.

"Now what?"

"I can't believe a woman with your looks has any trouble holding on to a man."

"Your assessment means so much to me." She couldn't believe she was having this conversation.

"A problem shared is a problem halved. Want to tell me about it?"

"Not at all, but thank you for your kind bedside manner."

"Ah, if you're going to start talking dirty, Doctor, I need to pull over."

"Huh?"

"Bed and all."

Abby blinked. Was that teasing note coming from the no-nonsense, dedicated surgeon, super doctor-stud Greg Hastings?

"Let me assure you I haven't the faintest idea of how to talk dirty or flirt. That's part of the problem. Not that I need to tell you any more. Good night, Doctor!"

"I'll call back. Persistence is one of my strong points."

She could think of a few other things to call it. "Why the interest? To feed the rumor mill?"

"Ah, thanks for your high regard. Actually I'm on a reconnaissance mission for Rose."

"Who will then feed the rumor mill?"

"I doubt it. She seems to attract information like a magnet does iron filings, but rarely spreads it—except to me, of course."

"Now you want to return the favor?"

"Actually, I'll admit to being curious myself."

"It's no big deal, and probably a very tired, familiar story. I thought there was more to a relationship than a certain man thought."

"Jeb Stuart."

Abby caught her breath. Greg was too sharp. "I didn't mention any names."

"I could feel the tension between the two of you at the banquet. And I have eyes. The woman he was with was a knockout. Hence the change of style on your part, I suspect."

"Which did nothing but make me look like an idiot."

"I don't know. I liked the dress."

Abby doggedly continued, ''I wanted a change, but obviously I don't have a clue about how to do it.''

''Do it?''

She blinked and frowned. ''Make the change.'' Heat flooded at the echo of his words. Suddenly she wondered what it would be like to do it with Greg Hastings. What would it be like to kiss him, have those surgeon's hands touch her intimately? Have his mouth cover her with passion? Pushing away the image, she frowned. Even fantasy had its limits, and this was one in which she dared not indulge. How would she ever face him at the hospital if she spent her free time daydreaming about the two of them together, intimately entwined?

It was warm in the apartment. She rose and walked to the window to crack it open a bit.

Intimate images refused to be dispelled, and began to dance in her mind again. Suddenly she envisioned him pursuing a reluctant female until she was totally captivated—just as Rose predicted.

''I guess I don't understand why you want a change. You're never going to look like that woman with Jeb last week. If that's his type, you don't have a chance.''

''I heard you have a reputation for blunt speaking. Thanks for offering hope.''

''False hope does no one any good. Are you hung up on Jeb Stuart?''

''Of course not! But I'm not exactly flooded with invitations for dates, either.'' She took a deep breath, deciding she knew where this was leading. ''Don't worry that you'll be coerced into taking me to the ball. I'll find someone by then!''

She closed her eyes. Had she really told him all that?

"You make it sound like a quest, or a challenge. I bet I could get you lined up with someone with no trouble."

"Great, another setup. I didn't like Dr. Taylor's solution, so I don't want yours. I have to go. Please forget we had this conversation."

She hung up the phone and headed for the bedroom. Even if he called back, she'd refuse to pick up. She'd had enough—and revealed far too much!

Only Carol had known why she felt uncertain around men. She'd been the only one to whom Abby had given the full details of her fiasco with Terry Bolton. She couldn't seem to shake the lasting anxiety in her own femininity that debacle had engendered. Well, not *anxiety* precisely. More distrust. Uncertainty. She didn't trust her own instincts anymore.

Getting ready for bed, she thought about Jeb. She'd misread that situation, obviously. But they'd been friends for so long. And when Carol died, they'd seem to become even closer. Nothing had ever been said, so when had she begun to assume they'd get married one day?

By Saturday, Abby's curiosity about Greg's sister's boutique had grown. Dressing casually in dark brown slacks and a cream blouse, she decided to spend the morning just browsing. For a few minutes she debated enlisting Kim's help, but decided against it. Somehow the dress Kim had talked her into hadn't been the success she'd hoped for.

She could hear the echo of Jeb's scathing comment.

Then she remembered what Greg had said. Maybe it hadn't been totally bad.

It was early when she reached Maiden Lane. None

of the trendy shops were yet opened. Passing time by gazing into the windows, Abby questioned what she was doing. Just because some arrogant man had suggested she try the boutique wasn't any real reason to do so. If she had her way, Dr. Greg Hastings would never know whether she had taken his advice or not. So why was she here?

The shop she stood in front of opened its doors. She checked her watch and headed back down the short street to the boutique. Finding it now open, she entered and was immediately impressed with its understated elegance. The place was larger than it looked from the small storefront, displaying suits, dresses and evening wear with loving care. To the right, frothy undergarments denoted the small lingerie section.

There were none of the tightly jammed racks she was used to in department stores. Here and there a few special dresses hung for ease in viewing, with mannequins displaying choice items.

Abby found herself gazing at a long, sultry slip dress in midnight-blue that whispered sex appeal. That's what she'd like to wear. But would it look as good on her as the mannequin?

Jeb's words echoed once again.

"Hello, may I help you?" A tall, slender woman appeared from the back. Her friendly smile relaxed Abby instantly.

"I'm just looking, thanks," she said, stepping to the rack nearest her. The silky feel of the blouses delighted her senses.

"Took my advice, I see." The masculine voice surprised her. She looked up—into Greg Hastings's amused eyes.

"What are you doing here?" Abby asked, surprised

to see him. She almost groaned aloud. So much for keeping her activities secret.

"I took Pam to breakfast. I dropped her off here and was ready to leave when I heard you."

Embarrassed to be caught, Abby nodded stiffly. "I was in the neighborhood and decided to see what she had."

"A friend of yours, Greg?" the other woman asked.

"Dr. Abby Trent, meet my sister, Pam Schuler."

"Ah, how do you do, Dr. Trent?" Pam smiled, glancing at her brother.

Abby knew he'd said something to his sister about her and wished she could just spin around and dash away. But that would be bad manners and she already had enough on her plate with Dr. Hastings.

"You have a lovely place," Abby said, trying to ignore the butterflies in her stomach. Why wouldn't the man just leave?

"Thank you. Anything special in mind?" Pam asked genially.

"No. Just browsing."

"Get her a few things for evening and all. And something for the ball, don't forget," Greg said irrepressibly.

"I can choose my own clothes, Dr. Hastings!"

"Mmm." His gaze roamed over her from the open neck of her blouse to the tip of her toes.

Abby raised her chin and turned away. "I think I'll come back another time."

"No, don't go," Pam said. Turning to her brother, she frowned at him. "Thanks for breakfast. Now if you don't want to ruin my business, take yourself away!"

"I'm not ruining anything."

"Go!"

"Maybe Dr. Trent would like me to stay."

Abby met his dancing eyes. "I don't care what you do, I have other errands." She turned as if to head for the door, feeling as foolish as a ten-year-old caught out spying on her older sister.

"Greg!" Pam said sharply.

"Okay, I'm going. This is the thanks I get for treating you to breakfast?"

"Next time you can drop me at the door. Goodbye!" Pam said, glaring at him.

"Dr. Trent, don't let Greg's teasing drive you away. I'd love for you to look around and see if there's anything you might like."

Pausing, Abby met Greg's gaze, noticing the deep brown of his eyes. They seemed richer, deeper—interested. In her? No one had been really interested in her since high school. Or if they had been, she'd shut them out.

Yet just a single look from Greg Hastings and she felt flushed with femininity; she felt sexy, almost desirable. She wanted to fuss with her hair, check that her lipstick was still bright, ask if he would help her pick out a dress. Something like what that mannequin wore.

He was still talking with his sister and Abby watched him, unable to look away. Just because his hair looked as if she should brush it back from his forehead was no reason for her fingers to tingle with yearning. Just because his dark eyes gleamed when they glanced at her was no reason to want to have him stay when she really wanted him gone. Just because his lower lip was slightly fuller than his top lip was no reason for her own to tremble and long to feel that sensuous mouth move against her own. So why did her gaze keep dropping to his lips? Why did she wonder what he would taste like?

She'd told herself to stop all fantasies about Greg Hastings. They were medical colleagues—nothing more!

When he looked at her, she blinked. She saw Pam looking at her expectantly. Had he said something she'd missed? Had she been caught examining him? Catching herself in the spell of his presence, she tried to ignore the sensations flooding her body. He radiated raw sex appeal. For the first time in her life Abby felt—almost alluring.

"What?"

"I told Pam I thought you were after a new look. I suspect you're tired of the reliable-doctor look in your free time," he said, daring her to contradict him.

She ignored him and nodded at Pam. "He's right, much as I hate to admit it. I would like a change."

"Something to help her attract the opposite sex," Greg added suggestively. The thought of transforming the quiet Dr. Trent into a *femme fatale* piqued his interest. And offered tantalizing possibilities. Maybe Rose's suggestion hadn't been so outlandish after all.

Glaring at him, Abby said, "Don't you have to leave? I thought your sister told you to go."

He almost laughed. "When you get to know me better, Abigail, you'll know I rarely do what I'm told unless I want to."

"I have no doubt about that," she mumbled.

Trying to defuse the growing tension, Pam walked over to one of the display racks and pulled out a lovely cinnamon-colored dress. "How about something like this for evening. It'll wear all day and still look fresh at night.''

"You ought to ask Rose for pointers on the dating scene. From what she tells me, she dates a different man every week," Greg added, leaning casually against a mirror, watching Abby's every move. If his sister really wanted him gone, he'd leave. But for now it was interesting to watch Abby's reactions.

"I don't need to talk to your secretary. I'll get my own experience, thank you." She regretted ever agreeing to Dr. Taylor's suggestion concerning an escort.

"I can just imagine the experience you'll get dating a lot of different men in San Francisco," he said dryly.

Abby raised her head. She wasn't planning to sleep with every man who took her out. But she didn't have to tell him that. She already regretted being so open with him, and coming to the boutique. She should have followed her first instincts and tossed the business card into the trash.

She'd made a mistake coming in the first place, and in staying so long.

"Greg, either help or get out," Pam said in frustration. "I have enough worries without you running off my clientele."

"Okay, I'll help," Greg said suddenly, amusement and something else in his expression.

"You will?" Pam asked. "That would be great. Exactly what kind of help are you talking about?"

"I'll help change our delectable Dr. Trent into the femme fatale she yearns to be." His gaze remained on Abby.

"Why ever would you do such a thing?" Abby asked, ignoring the sarcasm. She didn't need to be a femme fatale, just change enough that Jeb regretted destroying their friendship for the blond bombshell.

And maybe find her own date for the ball.

"So I'm not enlisted for escort duty at the last moment?" he asked whimsically.

Abby regarded him warily. "This may be a joke to you, but not to me."

Immediately his amusement fled. For a moment the cold, arrogant surgeon appeared. "I assure you I won't treat it as a joke. If you want some pointers, I'll give them to you. If not, say so and I'll leave just as Pam keeps trying to get me to do."

"What kind of pointers?" Suspicion grew as Abby tried to analyze why he'd make such an offer. It couldn't be because he didn't want to take her to the ball. All he had to do was say no.

He shrugged. "Whatever you don't know and want to about men."

"Well, that would fill a bookshelf!" Abby had never understood men.

"Are you serious, Greg?" Pam asked.

"We could try it and see. You game, Dr. Trent?"

Abby tried to see the pitfalls of such a crazy scheme. Greg already knew she didn't date, so there was no hiding that. She was committed to attending the conference and ball, her appointment to the committee had insured that. Could he help her? Or was it all some elaborate joke on his part?

Not that she'd ever heard Dr. Hastings was one for jokes. He was too cool, too reserved, too much a loner to go in for frivolity.

Which made his offer even more bizarre.

"I guess I could use some pointers," she said hesitantly.

His eyes stared into hers, holding her full attention. "The help would also include not only Pam, but my sister Elise, who is a very successful fashion model. Among the three of us we can give you everything you'd ever want."

His words sent a shiver up her spine. She didn't feel threatened, exactly, despite the aura of power that seemed to surge to the forefront. But she couldn't help imagining him wreaking havoc in her nice, orderly life.

Feeling awkward, Abby tried to think up something clever to say, but remained as tongue-tied as a young girl. "I appreciate your willingness to help me," she said formally. "But a few pointers would be all I'd need." Smiling at Pam, she added, "And some new clothes, maybe."

"Clothes will help, but you don't need much. You're a pretty woman, Doctor," Greg said bluntly.

Greg pushed away from the wall and stepped closer, his fingers brushing her hair.

"As for suggestions, I've got one right off the bat. Take this tawny-blond hair and lighten it up some with streaks of white blond, get it styled a little and you'll be a knockout. Your eyes are an unusual color, one moment almost green, another moment blue. With the proper clothes, you can make them your most compelling feature. Knock men off their feet. Especially if you flash them the smile that peeks out every once in a while."

You're a pretty woman. The last man to tell her that had been her father on her sixteenth birthday. And Terry a couple of times. But did she dare trust the words? Didn't men say one thing and mean something else entirely?

Abby felt the heat from Greg's body envelop hers. She took a breath, and his scent filled her nostrils, spicy and male. She licked dry lips and kept her gaze firmly on his, ignoring the overwhelming desire to step back and gain some distance, some perspective. He was so aggressively male!

Her thoughts whirling, she wondered if she was crazy to let herself even consider following through now that he had agreed.

As if he could read her mind, he leaned closer and cupped her chin in his hand, the warmth stealing into her skin, sweeping through her entire body. Mesmerized by the liquid heat in his eyes, she gazed up at him.

"Don't back out now, Abigail. We'll fix you up so good you'll have to beat the men off with a stick." Lightly his thumb grazed her lower lip.

The tingling awareness that swept through her from head to toes felt like a small electric shock. Her eyes locked with his and the boutique and his sister seemed to fade, disappearing into a gray mist. There were only the two of them, alone in the world, his breath against her cheeks and the odd, sensuous awareness that seemed to fill every pore.

She'd been dealing with men for years, first the cowboys on her dad's small ranch, then aspiring doctors, interns, residents and established physicians. But she'd never experienced such a strong physical reaction to any of them.

She had not expected him to touch her. Nor had she expected the flaring sensations that consumed her. What had she gotten herself into?

"Then let's start with the clothes," Pam said.

Abby blinked and seemed to come out of a trance.

She stepped away. How could she have been so mesmerized by the man? He and she didn't have a thing in common. Where was this physical awareness coming from?

"I really just came to look," Abby said, doing her best to ignore Greg, to ignore the clamoring of her senses for more of his touch, more of his attention. Remember his normal manner, she admonished herself. Today was the aberration. Usually he didn't know she existed.

Still not certain of his motives, she would wait and see how things unfolded. She was not trusting the man—not completely. But then, she didn't trust any man completely anymore. Not after her experience with Terry, and Jeb.

Chapter Four

By the time Abby returned home, she was excited about the clothes Pam had helped her choose. She had tried on dozens of dresses, skirts and blouses and casual wear. When they found the classical style that she liked, and suited her figure, Pam had brought several dresses into the dressing room that fit like a glove and enhanced the color of her eyes—just as Greg had predicted.

Frowning, she wondered how he'd known so much about women's attire and what would work. From his sisters? Or from women he dated?

Trying on one of the dresses again, she loved the feel of the soft silk against her skin. When the doorbell rang, she debated taking off the dress before answering, but that would take too long.

"Oh, that's beautiful. Where did you get it?" Kim asked when Abby opened the door.

"Come in and see what else I got," Abby said, glad to share her new purchases.

Kim raved over everything, then tilted her head and looked at Abby.

"There's something different about you. What is it?"

"The clothes, I guess. Nothing else has changed."

"Maybe. But there's something." Kim studied her for a moment then gave up. "I think the dress we bought wasn't quite right."

"It was a pretty dress, just not for me. Would you like it? It's only been worn once." And the memories of that night insured she'd never wear it again!

"Sure, if you don't want it. You need to do something with your makeup and hair next," Kim said, "to go with the new clothes."

"Someone suggested I get some highlights," Abby said slowly as she drew the dress over her head. Donning jeans and a casual top, she looked at her friend. "What do you think?"

"I think you'd be a knockout. Can doctors do that?"

Abby laughed. "What, get their hair streaked?"

"No, start looking fabulous."

Warmed by her friend's enthusiasm, Abby laughed at the nonsense. "Afraid all my baby patients will distrust my skills?"

"I guess not. Wait until Jeb sees you. He'll have a fit and dump Sara like a hot potato."

Abby paused as she hung up another new dress. "I hope not."

"What? Did I miss something?" Kim asked in mock surprise as she handed Abby another dress.

"Actually," she said, turning toward Kim, "I don't want Jeb."

Kim sat on the bed and stared at her. "I thought that was what all this was about," she said, waving her hand around.

"At first. But I've been thinking about it and now I don't want Jeb to change a thing."

Kim's eyes narrowed as if she were deep in thought. "Another man?"

"Hardly," Abby scoffed. But despite her best efforts, the image of Greg Hastings rose. She frowned and resumed her task. She wasn't even sure she liked the man. She didn't trust his motives in offering help, and she sure didn't want to be reminded he'd been her escort at one of the most embarrassing events of her life.

Yet...

Making plans with Kim to go out Sunday afternoon to the movies, Abby finished putting away her things and, once her friend left, prepared a light dinner.

She no longer wanted to knock Jeb off his feet, but the thought of changing her image made her sparkle. It was past time. She'd spent all the years since the end of her relationship with Terry devoted to studying to become a doctor. Now that she'd achieved her goal, it was time to branch out and see what else life had to offer.

Monday flew by with extra appointments squeezed in for those children who had become ill over the weekend.

Tuesday was a disaster. One of Abby's patients was given the wrong medicine and had an immediate allergic reaction. While she responded to that, appointments stacked up.

Then she spilled coffee on a brand-new skirt and her lab coat and walked around feeling damp all afternoon. Twice she lost her train of thought when listening to consulting physicians regarding treatment for critical patients, and had to ask them to repeat themselves. Both times the frustrated physicians grew sarcastic, asking if she really wanted to listen to them, or would prefer daydreaming for some new and more effective way of treating patients?

It was raining when she left the hospital, and she had neither coat nor umbrella. Her car was parked far from the entrance and she was soaked by the time she reached it. To top it off, her period started and she felt achy and cranky.

She arrived home tired, wet and disgusted with everything. Maybe she wasn't cut out to deal with sarcastic, unsympathetic male doctors or to live alone in the city. She'd never had such a rotten day at home. Maybe she should have returned to Yreka and opened a private practice there. Small towns in northern California always needed physicians.

A quick warm shower went a long way toward making her feel better, but she was still slightly depressed and feeling weepy. If she'd been home, her mom and dad would take pains to cheer her up. She'd have the ranch animals to take care of, to take her mind off all the mistakes and stress and sardonic comments. But here she was alone, feeling dumb, clumsy and down. Some of it had to be because of the weather. Who expected rain in San Francisco in May?

Unable to settle on any one thing during the evening, Abby waited impatiently until she thought she could go to sleep. Bedtime couldn't come too early.

Changing into her nightgown, she was just about to climb into bed when the phone rang.

"Abigail?"

"Yes." It was Greg Hastings. "Is something wrong?" Why was he calling her so late? Or, more appropriately, why was he calling at all?

"Are you all right? Your voice sounds funny."

"Of course I'm fine." Immediately classifying the incidents of the day as minor annoyances, she sat down, ready to duel with Dr. Hastings.

"Rumor has it Dr. Peters was less than congenial over the bed of that liver patient."

"Trust the rumor mill to have picked up on that. And it was Jesse Mitchell. He's my patient but not responding to treatment. I thought Dr. Peters might help. Rose, I suppose," she said, resigned to the far-flung reach of hospital gossip.

"Naturally. What happened?"

Abby told him about the incident, and then expanded to include her entire day, embellishing each incident, making sure he understood the appalling gaffes she'd made with the other doctors, all the time wearing a lab coat with a huge coffee stain on it. She wasn't sure, but once or twice she thought she heard Greg chuckle. That was as far as she could go to dispel the rumors.

"Are you laughing at me, Doctor?" she asked suspiciously, her spirits inexplicably rising.

"And if I were?"

"I'll have you know these were serious incidents."

"Right, and I have a bridge to sell you."

"I know, the Golden Gate."

"Right. I called about the conference."

"At eleven o'clock at night? Couldn't it wait until I was at work?"

"I tried work, three times today."

"Oh." She thought about the small stack of pink phone messages waiting on her desk. She'd had her secretary pull any urgent ones, and every one relating to her patients. The rest she'd left to deal with tomorrow.

"It was a hectic day, sorry I didn't get back to you." She bet he ran his life with more order. Did he ever have to wait until the next day to return calls?

"No problem. We can talk now, unless I'm keeping you up."

"I was ready for bed," she said without thinking, then could have bitten her tongue. It felt strange to talk to him wearing only her nightgown. But there was no reason he had to know what she was wearing.

Idly she wondered if she could sound seductive and sexy on the phone. Not that she'd ever try such a thing with Greg Hastings!

"Are you wearing some prissy long white virginal gown?" he said, his voice suddenly rough.

She frowned. How had he known that? Was that her image? Prissy and virginal? No, quiet and mousy. Is that what mousy women wore? No wonder she needed to change her image. No woman of thirty wanted to be thought of as prissy and virginal!

She didn't answer right away. He thought he was so smart. Could she shake that assurance a little? Show him she wasn't as predictable as he thought? Without further thought, she blurted out, "Actually I'm wearing a cream-colored silk teddy. It is cut really high on the sides. It's plunging in front and back and covered in lots of sheer lace with tiny straps that I hope will hold it up during the night." She'd seen the teddy at Pam's, but never in her life imagined wearing such a frilly concoction. Still, Greg didn't need to know that.

His groan was clear across the telephone wire.

"What are you wearing?" she asked, hoping the laughter in her voice wasn't transmitted.

"Nothing. Not a stitch."

Liquid heat coursed through her instantly as she pictured his powerful, sexy body lying on white sheets. She knew his shoulders were wide, his chest muscles hard, with no extra flab anywhere. She blinked. Raised on a ranch, and trained as a doctor, she had a healthy understanding of the human body and procreation. She could picture Greg, and her breathing became difficult.

"Abby?" His low voice reverberated gently against her ear.

"What?" she said, glad he couldn't see her. Why had she thought she could sound sexy on the phone? Just the thought of him on the other end of the line naked in bed was shattering her equilibrium.

"I wish I could see you in that teddy." The velvet tones wrapped around her, heated her, excited her.

She prudently kept quiet.

"Abby? Are you still there?"

"Yes, but not for long. Good night, Greg."

She hung up the phone while she had an ounce of strength left. Pulling the covers up to her chin, she tried to sleep, but the picture in her mind refused to let her relax. Over and over she imagined him making love to her. She knew it would be glorious!

She seemed to know how his hands would feel on her bare skin. She knew they would be hot and electric against her breasts, her belly, her thighs. His body would be hard, sculpted with muscles. Her own hands would trace their outlines, learn his particular shape. Her mouth could explore his skin and learn his taste as he'd be learning hers.

With a groan, she rolled over and pulled a pillow on top of her head. Now she was driving herself crazy.

It rained Wednesday and Thursday and Abby was afraid it would continue through the weekend. She caught glimpses of Greg several times through the rest of the week, though they never had a moment to talk, and he'd never told her why he'd called about the committee.

Friday night when Abby turned the key in the door to her apartment, she wanted nothing more than a hot bath, a quick dinner and bed. She was exhausted! She'd had two difficult cases in the past two days and one emergency at three in the morning.

She had gone directly to work after the emergency and put in a full day. The uncommonly long hours proved difficult, though she usually loved her job. She had worked hard for a long time to attain her present position and wasn't about to complain about the downside—though she was tempted. It was times like today that she especially missed Carol. And Jeb.

In earlier times, she would have called them. The three of them would have gathered at their favorite pizza restaurant and regaled each other with the trauma of practicing medicine. Sharing problems always made them seem lighter.

But those days were forever gone.

Kicking off her shoes, she wandered into the bedroom and collapsed on her bed. It was a wide four-poster, covered with a colorful quilt and a mound of pillows. Closing her eyes, she relaxed completely. Long, slow minutes slid by, then, worried she'd fall asleep still fully dressed, she forced herself up and into a bath.

Later, dressed in her most comfortable faded jeans and a loose cotton top, her hair still drawn into a high ponytail from bathing, she fixed a quick omelette for dinner. Revived by her bath and dinner, Abby turned on the television. It was something to while away the hours until bed. She was sleepy—it wouldn't be long.

When the doorbell sounded, Abby turned down the volume on the television and went to see who it was. She wasn't expecting anyone. It could be Kim, though she usually had a date on Friday nights.

Or Jeb?

No, surely he'd be out with Sara.

Greg Hastings was the last person she expected to find standing in the hall when she opened the door.

He wasn't wearing a suit, but dressed comfortably in dark slacks and a baggy tweed sweater. Obviously he'd been home and changed. What was he doing here?

"Hi. Busy?" he asked, stepping inside uninvited, a briefcase in one hand.

Abby frowned and closed the door. She wore no makeup, her hair was pulled back and she had on her oldest clothes. What a way to make an impression on one of Merrimac's leading physicians. Despite everything, she was unable to stop the exhilaration that slammed into her at his unexpected visit. She wished she had known he was coming. She would have worn something a little more impressive! Brushed her hair, put on makeup.

"I'm watching TV. I didn't expect you." She

hadn't missed an appointment, had she? Frowning, she tried to remember. Not that she'd ever forgotten one thing about Greg Hastings. She'd certainly have remembered scheduling a meeting with him!

He ran one finger across her forehead, smoothing out the frown lines. "Don't do that, you'll wrinkle. We never reviewed the committee work I called about the other night. I took a chance you'd be home tonight. Can we go over it now?"

She ignored the undercurrents of attraction that swirled. She was tired, that was all.

But the thought struck her that while she was home alone on a Friday night, obviously Dr. Hastings had no plans for the evening, either. Especially if he wanted to work! For some reason that made her wonder even more about the man.

She stepped back from his touch, feeling the heat of his body, which seemed to envelop her. Her stomach tightened and she dropped her gaze, frowning anew at the unexpected reaction. She seemed flushed with instant, rampant awareness. Her nerve endings resonated from his touch, clamored for more. She felt the stirring of unknown feelings deep within her and her breasts began to ache and tingle, yearning to be stroked, touched.

She swallowed hard, unable to move, yet needing to gain some control before she made a fool of herself.

She'd never been so keenly aware of another person before, never so conscious of sensations that deluged her at a man's touch. If she knew better how to manage the male of the species, she could cope. But now it drove her crazy. Greg's lightest touch evoked sensations almost forgotten. Raised longings that she'd once dreamed about before Terry had shattered her trust. Before she'd wildly imagined she and Jeb would build a future together. She was batting a thousand in the wrong vibes' department. Time to get control of her senses before they led her astray once more!

His touch lingered as if he'd traced patterns of fire and ice on her skin. Her heart tripped in her chest, beat so fast she wondered if he noticed. Sheesh, he'd come to discuss business and she was going off the deep end.

Yearning for the unattainable was not too bright. Hadn't she learned that lesson before?

Suddenly she wanted to step closer, demand he wrap his arms around her and hold her tightly. Strip her from head to toe and touch her all over. Take her chances the future would be different from the past.

This was about the conference, not *them!* she reminded herself.

"If it's so important you needed to come on a Friday evening, I can spare the time," she said, leading the way into the living room.

She sank onto the edge of one of the Queen Anne chairs, trying to hide her reactions. She watched as he casually sat on the love seat, as at ease in the elegantly furnished living room as he'd appeared at the hospital. Against the dainty, feminine furniture, his strong masculinity looked all the more virile. Abby couldn't take her eyes off him, amazed at where her thoughts led. Was his very proximity starting to affect her brain?

He looked quizzical. "I like your hair that way."

She grinned, the tense mood shattering. If he could joke about her hair, there was nothing hidden in his visit. More's the pity.

He snapped open his briefcase and withdrew a

folder. Spreading it open on the coffee table, he looked at her, his dark eyes enigmatic.

"Don't you think if you sat beside me you could see better?"

Feigning a nonchalance she didn't feel, Abby moved to sit as far from him on the narrow love seat as she could, hoping she wasn't being too obvious. She leaned forward to study the sheets of papers he spread out, conscious every second of how dangerously close Greg was. His dark pants hugged his thighs. The baggy sweater looked disreputable and seductive at the same time. His hair didn't have that immaculately groomed look, appearing more like he'd repeatedly run his fingers through it.

She scrutinized the papers, wishing she could decipher what they said. But her mind seemed to have stalled. She shivered in confusion. Did all women feel like this around him?

"You're hard to reach at the hospital. I wanted Rose to get started on the final list of invitees and corporate sponsors. I thought you might be busy Monday."

He smiled at her and Abby was lost. It was the dimple. Or the flashing brown eyes.

She felt comfortable discussing medical techniques, prognoses of patients, even the price of cattle because of her dad's ranch. But not flirting with a virile, sexy doctor whose very look seemed to melt all her inhibitions and resistance.

"But not busy tonight?"

He glanced at her indignant expression. Was that amusement she saw reflected? "Not at all. If tonight is not convenient, I can come back another time. Or we can meet at the hospital. But I wanted to get Rose started first thing Monday morning."

She wished she could have mentioned a dozen previous engagements. But it was obvious she'd been set for a night at home. With as much dignity as she could muster, she picked up the top sheet, trying to focus on the names. She was making a fool of herself. Concentrate and he'd be gone soon!

But the thought surfaced again and again that it would be the perfect opportunity to practice flirting. Kim would have done so in a heartbeat. Even Carol would have been a lot more friendly, and she'd been engaged.

Sadly Abby realized even though she didn't trust the man fully, she wanted to push the limits. Test her own abilities, and see where they led her.

Just for practice.

Yet the legacy Terry Bolton and Jeb Stuart left was not easily ignored. Intellectually she knew she should try again. But it proved difficult—impossible with this man!

No matter how peculiar she felt whenever she was around him—giddy and hot and…and bothered— wouldn't he laugh if he ever suspected?—she couldn't bring herself to flirt.

"What's this part?" she asked, as one brief paragraph jumped out at her.

"Where?" He leaned closer, following her finger.

"As co-chairs we have to introduce the VIPs at the ball? And report the total amount that is received?"

"Scratch that. It was suggested but I vetoed it. You'll have the night to spend with your date."

He was mocking her.

"You're worried I won't come up with a date, aren't you?" she blurted out.

"No. If nothing else, I'm sure Ben Taylor will—"

She held up a hand, palm out. "Stop. I will not go with you! I'll manage fine on my own."

He shrugged. "If you say so." Eyeing her speculatively, he murmured, "I could help, I guess."

"By doing what?"

"Pam's been on my case to come up with those pointers I promised. Even Rose—"

"Oh, please! You aren't discussing my personal life with everyone you meet, are you?" She jumped up, scattering the papers when she knocked against the table. "I can't believe this!"

He leaned back on the cushions and watched her pace the narrow space. "Correct me if I'm wrong, but until recently you spent a lot of time studying. Then you and that Jeb Stuart were a duo. Now that he's with someone else, you're at loose ends."

She spun around and glared at him. "It's not quite what you think. Carol and Jeb and I were great friends. All through school we did everything together. The three of us. There wasn't anything romantic between Jeb and me."

He raised an eyebrow in disbelief.

She crossed her arms and rubbed her hands over them to get warm. "Carol's death left us numb." Not for a million dollars would she tell him she'd mistaken Jeb's comforting as something more.

"Now we're both moving on with our lives."

"So do you want help meeting some men or not?" Greg asked.

"Cut to the chase, is that right?"

"I prefer to think of it as cutting to the heart of the matter. I don't have time to waste on a lot of dancing around the issue."

She'd heard the rumors about how coolly efficient

Dr. Hastings was. He treated the disease efficiently, but his bedside manner left something to be desired.

And now she was seeing him in action.

"So you'll play matchmaker and set me up with someone?" she asked, embarrassment threatening to consume her. How had she come to this?

She felt light-headed. It was hard to follow the conversation. She wanted to demand he leave, yet some part of her was curious enough to want to see it through. See what he came up with.

"I know a few men who are interested in meeting someone new. And who will be intrigued with that air of innocence you portray so well."

She stiffened at his words, meeting his eyes. She *was* innocent. Was that a crime?

"So what do I do?" she grumbled—all the more aware of her shortcomings in this realm. And aware of the longings she didn't know how to control. And shouldn't feel to begin with. She couldn't seem to keep her eyes off him. Intrigued by the way he moved, so smoothly and in control. The way his eyes would crinkle a little in the corners when he laughed.

And of course that smile was enough to turn her knees to Jell-O.

She was not getting involved with Greg Hastings! He certainly would not be one of the men intrigued by her air of innocence so well portrayed.

"You seem nervous, is something wrong?" he asked. His amusement was blatant.

She wasn't fooled. She could tell by the tone of voice he knew damn well something was wrong. And probably precisely what!

"No. Let's get the rest of this conference matter cleared up. I'm tired and wanted an early night."

"I could come back tomorrow," he offered.

And have a second session trying to fight the urge to ask him to kiss her? To touch him and see if that tingling all over would fade, or grow stronger? Another time to resist becoming a babbling idiot in his presence. She didn't think so.

"Let's finish tonight."

"However long it takes, right?"

She blinked and nodded. When his gaze ran down the length of her, she shivered and hastened to gather the scattered papers, hoping to regain a modicum of composure. She was a mature woman, not some giddy teenager.

Tell that to her hormones, she grumbled silently. Had someone invented an inoculation against sexual attraction for arrogant, cynical surgeons?

Maybe she should suggest it as a new medical project.

Chapter Five

She was driving him crazy and she didn't have a clue! They concluded the work he'd devised and Greg watched Abby stack the papers they'd reviewed. She seemed distant and annoyed. He was to blame, not that he felt a morsel of regret. With an impatient gaze he watched as she tidied the papers and slipped them into the folder.

He'd never suspected she'd look so great in jeans. The stretch of denim across her rounded bottom when she leaned over to pick up a fallen sheet was tantalizing. She was alluring without even realizing it. He'd never met a woman so unaware of her own sex appeal as Abigail Trent.

He had difficulty believing she didn't have any idea what effect she had. She was a doctor, for heaven's sake. She knew as much about human anatomy as he did. How could she not suspect she was driving him insane?

Yet there was the tantalizing air of innocence that had him puzzled.

Which was the real woman? He'd had experience with women over the years. From his ex-wife to his sisters' friends. And the nurses who threw themselves at him as Rose so often remarked.

Yet he hadn't felt this need for a particular woman before. He reached out to close the briefcase, startled at his thoughts. *He wanted Abigail Trent.* He wanted to strip that shirt off and kiss her all over her warm satiny skin. He wanted to see her beneath him, her blond hair spread out like a soft cloud all around her face, see what color her eyes were when she was in the midst of passion. Would they be green, blue, or something in between?

It wouldn't take much from her to ignite fires that couldn't be banked down. He'd thought about her constantly over the past few days, while he'd deliberately refrained from contacting her. Deliberately forced himself to stay away. She was either playing some convoluted game, or was as innocent as a newborn. He hadn't figured out which yet, but she acted unlike anyone he'd met in the past decade.

Slowly he'd come to the determination to find out if she was truly naive, or leading him on. Either way, he would cut to the chase. If she was playing some game, it wouldn't hurt to stretch it out a bit. If she was truly as innocent as she sometimes appeared, he needed to take his time and make sure he didn't scare her away by rushing his fences.

One way or another, he planned to find out.

Not that he was interested in any long-term entanglement. Michelle had cured him once and for all of any idea a doctor could maintain a marriage in the face of his duties. And his work was of paramount importance to him.

Women didn't like their husbands to be called away at a moment's notice—usually at the precise moment it was time to sit down at an important dinner party they'd worked on for weeks, or in the middle of the night when the wife had expected her husband's full attention.

Michelle's vitriolic complaints about him as a husband and provider still echoed eight years after he'd seen the last of her.

But he wasn't looking for a life partner—just to assuage the hunger that was building when he came around Abby.

He shifted, suddenly uncomfortable. If he didn't get his mind off the image of her beneath him in a tumbled bed, he'd do something stupid. And he hadn't done anything stupid in a long time. Maybe a few nights together would be enough to get her out of his system.

"We're finished, right?" she asked.

He looked at her, wishing she'd smile like she did in staff meetings. He'd like to see the sunny expression that she shared so freely with others and rarely sent his way.

"Kicking me out?" he asked. Glancing at his watch, he noticed it wasn't that late. Surely she could ask him to stay for a while.

"I thought you'd have something else to do."

"Nothing. Now is as good a time as any for you to tell me what you'd like in a man."

"Excuse me?"

"So I'll know who to introduce you to." When he was good and ready.

"That's just dumb. I can find my own date for the ball!"

He shrugged. "We're not just talking about the hospital ball. You don't want my sister bugging me all the time because I didn't help expand your social life, do you?"

She sighed, the move pressing her breasts against the soft cotton of her shirt.

"I don't have any special idea about what I'd like in a man," she said, sitting stiffly on the chair halfway across the room.

"Doctors okay?"

"Why not?"

"I don't think practicing medicine and a family life go together," he said slowly.

"That's dumb. Most doctors are married."

"Not so dumb. I was married myself once. It didn't work out."

Her obvious surprise startled him. If she didn't know that basic fact, maybe he was reading her wrong. Maybe she truly wasn't interested in him, and not playing some game.

"What happened?" she asked.

"She didn't want to compete with medicine."

"So because of that, you shut yourself up like a monk?"

"Hardly. But I've been down that road and it led nowhere. I'm not in the market for a wife."

"So no kids, either?"

"If I don't have time for a wife, how good a father would I make?"

She shook her head. "It's a question of priorities. You make your family a priority."

"I think medicine's a priority."

Growing pensive, she shrugged. "I hope to get married one day. And maybe I should think about it soon. Carol's death really shook me up. She was young, vibrant, so alive. Then suddenly she was gone. She'll never get married, never have those children she so wanted. Life is uncertain. I'm afraid sometimes I'll end up dead at a young age, like Carol."

"All the more reason to grab what you want while you can."

Slowly she smiled. "Right. Maybe I'll take you up on the offer to introduce me to some men looking to expand their horizons."

"Right, you don't want to waste any time." She didn't have to look so happy at the thought of meeting other men.

"I'm thirty. If I want a family, I had better get started."

"And medicine? It'll take a back seat?"

"No, but unlike you, I think I can balance both. I want to experience all the fullness life has to offer. In a way, I feel I'm doing it for Carol as well as for me."

A few years of reality would dim the stars in her eyes, force her to recognize the limitations a dedicated physician faced, Greg thought. Was that some of the appeal she held? Her shining optimism in face of his cynicism?

"Who are you going to introduce me to first?" she asked almost eagerly.

"I'll think about it over the weekend and let you know." There were several men he knew who were looking for someone to establish a lasting relationship with. For a moment he regretted making the offer. He wasn't ready to turn her loose on an unsuspecting world.

"So if you're not going to kick me out immediately, want to watch this movie?" he asked, gesturing to the muted TV. "It started a few minutes ago and is one I saw several years ago and liked."

"Sure." She turned up the sound and began watching it as if there would be a detailed quiz later.

So much for her making some kind of play for him. Yet the thought struck that the pursuit would prove to be all the more interesting for her indifference. Or was that the allure—her indifference after years of having women try to gain his interest?

Greg rose some time later and clicked off the television. He watched Abby as she slept in the chair. Her head rested against the side, her hand relaxed in her lap. Wryly he admitted he obviously wasn't the male hunk Rose kept telling him he was. His hostess had fallen asleep!

When he called her name, she blinked and opened her eyes, staring around her in puzzlement.

"Oh, no, did I fall asleep? I'm so sorry!" She sat up, stretching slowly. The movement outlined her slim form and had his hands itching to trace that silhouette.

"My fault," Greg said easily. "I shouldn't have stayed when I saw you were tired. Walk me to the door and lock up. You'll be in bed in just a few minutes."

He turned away and picked up his briefcase, wishing his imagination wasn't running in overdrive. The thought of her in bed, wearing that impossible teddy, had him growing aroused and antsy. They didn't know each other well enough for her to invite him to stay, but he wanted to.

She stood up, her eyes on his baggy tweed sweater as if she couldn't quite meet his gaze. She apologized again.

"Hey." He tilted her face up to his, the softness of her skin like silk against his fingertips. She'd be this satiny all over, he knew.

"It's no problem. A blow to my ego, that's all. I never knew I was so boring."

She flushed. "Oh, that makes it even worse. I'm sorry."

Without thinking, he dropped a light kiss against her lips.

Her eyes widened and her gaze locked with his. It took all his strength to step back and not pull her into his arms for a real kiss.

Damn, Greg thought wryly as he turned and headed directly for the door before he forgot all rules of civilized behavior and swept her off her feet and into her bedroom.

He'd never had a woman fall asleep on him before. He should have been annoyed, instead he didn't want to leave. He'd wanted to stay. More importantly he had wanted her to want him to stay. Didn't she feel that same sexual pull of attraction? Or to her was he just a colleague from the hospital she felt comfortable enough around to fall asleep?

He was right, it was a blow to his ego. One he made plans to insure never occurred again!

Abby turned off the lights in a daze. Had Dr. Demigod Hastings actually kissed her? Or had she still been dreaming?

She didn't like his type. In her opinion, doctors should be warm, caring individuals; instead, Greg seemed to treat medicine as if it were a craft and a business. She'd noticed he never called patients by name—always by what was wrong with them. The gall bladder. The ruptured spleen.

His patients were people. Didn't he realize that?

Still, he did great work and had a tremendous recovery rate. Some said he had magic in his hands. If she ever had a patient who needed surgery, she'd recommend Greg.

Brushing her teeth a few minutes later, she gazed at her reflection. Her hair drooped to one side, the haphazard ponytail almost a thing of the past. She looked tired. But the sparkle in her eyes surprised her. She hadn't really *liked* that kiss, had she?

She held her breath a moment then exhaled slowly. Not only had she liked it, she was afraid she wanted another one. A real mouths-open, tongues-touching, body-pressed-together kiss.

"Forget it!" she told herself. The last thing she needed was to get some sort of fixation on Greg Hastings! Besides, hadn't he just told her he'd fix her up with someone else?

Which also didn't make a bit of sense. Why would he even think of such a thing, much less volunteer to help?

Unless he had been so horrified at escorting her to the banquet he wanted to make sure it never happened again.

Climbing into bed a bit later, Abby vowed she'd do what she had to in order to find someone she could invite to the ball. There was no way she wanted Dr. Hastings or Ben Taylor to see her as needing help.

She was bright, intelligent, and passably pretty. The specter of Terry Bolton and her own commitment to studying medicine had kept her from testing her wings as a woman. But that was in the past, and was no proof she couldn't succeed.

Just before she fell asleep, she wished once again things were as they had been for the past ten years. She missed Jeb and Carol terribly.

Saturday morning Abby swept through her apartment like a whirlwind. Living alone, it didn't take much to get it clean. The afternoon loomed ahead of her, and she spontaneously called Kim's hair salon to see if they could squeeze her in for a haircut—and if she gathered the nerve, she'd have it streaked, as well.

Surprised to find she could drop in, she grabbed her purse and was ready to walk out the door when the phone rang.

"Abigail, Greg here. Are you free for dinner tonight?" his rich voice answered her greeting.

"Dinner?" Her heart began pounding again.

"We can discuss our plan."

"Our plan?" She was beginning to feel like a parrot. "What plan?"

"We didn't get a lot of time to discuss what you're looking for in a companion. I thought we could do so over dinner tonight. Do you like seafood? We'll eat at the Wharf. I'll pick you up at seven."

"I don't think—"

"Oops, gotta run, my pager just went off."

Without another word, he hung up.

"—we need to go to that extent," she finished slowly to the dial tone. She replaced the receiver. Greg wanted to have dinner with her tonight? To discuss what she wanted in a date?

Glaring at the phone, she realized she didn't have his phone number. There was no way to call him back, unless she tried the hospital. But she shied away from that idea. If he wasn't in, she couldn't ask for his number—not without expecting the news to be all over the hospital in no time.

She could ignore the call. See if Kim was free and make sure she wasn't home at seven.

Yet the thought of going to dinner with Greg was tantalizing. They were colleagues, nothing more. Maybe if she got to know him a bit better the unsettling sensation that swamped her every time they were together would fade.

Some small feminine part of her also wanted to show him she wasn't the misfit she feared he thought her.

Abby took extra pains getting ready that evening. She loved the way her hair looked. Taking Greg's advice, she'd had it streaked, then trimmed. It cascaded down across her shoulders, the waves and curls soft and feminine, looking like gossamer with the highlights she'd acquired that afternoon.

She admitted grudgingly that his suggestion had been a good one. Somehow she didn't like the fact, but there was no denying it suited her. And it was nothing like the outrageous style Kim had manufactured last week.

She felt special. And buoyed up. Surprised, she realized she was looking forward to matching wits with Dr. Hastings that evening.

The frosty blue dress she had bought at Pam's boutique deepened the blue in her eyes and highlighted the delicate pink tint in her cheeks. It was short and sassy—skimming her knees. Her high heels displayed her shapely legs to full advantage, and gave her some extra height. She looked nothing like the conservative doctor in her white coat.

Now if she only could think of scintillating conversation with which to enthrall her escort. Laughing at her nonsense, she went into the living room to wait for Greg.

He arrived promptly at seven. Abby threw open the door as soon as she heard him.

"A new look," he said, as his gaze skimmed across her from the top of her curls to her fancy shoes, lingering an extra second at the bodice of her dress and the short hemline.

Abby flushed. There was something decidedly sexy about a man's perusal. She felt more feminine than ever in her life. Taking a deep breath, she smiled brightly. No reason he needed to suspect how uncertain she felt. Those fluttering nerves would calm down eventually, wouldn't they?

"I'm ready, just let me get my coat." She flicked a glance over him, noting how his dark suit fit perfectly. The snowy white shirt emphasized his sexy masculinity. The polish on his shoes shone like a mirror. Her heart skipped a beat. She wondered what she was doing going out with this man. She suddenly felt daring and reckless and quite different from a dedicated doctor.

And totally out of her league!

When they reached the restaurant on the water, Greg ushered her inside. The maître d' nodded as soon as Greg gave his name, and asked them to follow him. As they wound their way through the linen-covered tables, Abby noticed how crowded the restaurant was, not surprising for a Saturday night. They were lucky they didn't have to wait.

They seemed to be heading toward the huge floor-to-ceiling windows that provided a picture-postcard view of San Francisco Bay and the Golden Gate Bridge, now silhouetted against the waning sun.

Seated, they ordered and in only moments the waiter returned with the wine Greg had selected. Gratefully Abby sipped the delicious zinfandel, relishing the taste, glad to have something to do. So far she wasn't exactly entertaining her escort. Somewhere between her apartment and the restaurant she'd become almost tongue-tied. A normal occurrence around Greg. And something she had to overcome.

The waiter appeared with their salads. With a bow, he placed them on the table. Maybe she could keep her mouth so full of food Greg wouldn't expect her to talk, she thought desperately, reaching for the salad fork.

"Now that you've been on staff for a few months and settled in, how do you like Merrimac General?" he asked.

Feeling on safe ground, Abby relaxed marginally and began to tell him how much she enjoyed working at the hospital, how she was gradually finding her way around, and beginning to build a patient list. She asked him a few questions about his specialty and before she knew it, dinner was finished. It had proved easier than she'd thought. But they still hadn't touched on the reason he'd asked her out.

"Something for dessert?" Greg asked.

Shaking her head, she reached for her wineglass again. She didn't normally drink much wine, or much of anything else, either. But this was delicious, and she had relaxed as the meal progressed.

As she took a sip, her gaze met his. Abby was unable to look away. She stared back, feeling excited at the intensity in his eyes. A tiny flame curled and flickered within. She longed to draw a deep breath and break the spell, yet couldn't bring herself to do so.

"Ready to discuss our plan?" he asked.

Just when she was beginning to feel almost comfortable, she thought, frowning.

"*Our* plan?"

"You want to start dating as soon as possible, right? We wouldn't want any delays in getting you that big date for the hospital ball." His voice sounded bland, smooth. Yet it raised her hackles.

"Once again I might remind you, Doctor, that this is really not your concern. I assure you I won't let Dr. Taylor coerce you into escorting me. The ball is totally different from the banquet. I think I can manage on my own. I don't need help from you!"

"You don't want to be on your own for the great American date search. And if you're interested in meeting a man, you want something to last, right?"

She shrugged, not planning to give him any more ammunition. It was bad enough as it was.

"Come to think of it, I could be doing a disservice to the men of this city. Why should I assist you in snaring one of them?"

"Snaring? A date to the ball isn't a marriage proposal."

"Who knows where a first date can lead."

She shrugged. "Not all men view marriage like it's the plague. Aren't you interested in settling down and sharing your life with someone special?"

His expression grew grim. "As I told you, I've been there, done that."

"And never plan to do so again, right? Marriage and medicine don't mix."

"You've got it."

"And you think I want a cynic finding me a date? That would be a great match. I'm sorry your own marriage didn't work, but that doesn't mean others won't."

"Don't be sorry, we are much better apart than we ever were together. At least I am. And I learned that lesson at a young age. You still have that ahead of you."

She thought about Terry and the humiliation she'd once thought she'd never recover from. Then Jeb and the foolish dreams she'd begun to weave. She would not make those mistakes again. This time she'd do it right, make sure she and someone special had common interests and common goals. Guard her heart until she knew for sure.

"You don't know that," she said, arguing softly.

"Ever the optimist?"

"Maybe. Anyway," she said, "I have to take what you say with a grain of salt. Thank goodness not all men think that way."

"Only the smart ones."

"So now I'm looking for some dumb guy?" she said, trying to lighten the tone of the conversation. She felt embarrassed enough without having to defend her view of marriage to a cynic.

"Maybe he wouldn't totally be out of his mind to hook up with you. Do you want to marry another doctor?"

"I thought we were talking about dating! You're getting me married off already?"

"You've got permanence and heart and flowers written all over you. So do you want me to introduce you to some doctors?"

"Not especially, one in the family would be enough, don't you think? I mean, the hours are killers, never knowing when we'll be called out. And doctors can be so arrogant."

"Present company excepted, of course."

She laughed. "I doubt it. For either you or me. Goes with the territory sometimes, don't you think? Anyway, with my luck, I'd fall for an obstetrician and you know they're never home at night."

"Okay, doctors are out. How about a stockbroker?"

"I'm really not setting out requirements. Don't you think I should just see who wants to ask me out?"

"In this day and age women don't have to wait."

"I do," she said softly.

"Ah, an old-fashioned girl?" That husky voice danced over her like warm syrup, making her almost dizzy with the sweet sensations that seeped in.

"Sort of." The way he said it made it sound so naive. But she wasn't ready to call up a strange man and invite him out, no matter how old-fashioned that made her.

She felt distracted by Greg's eyes, enveloped by the heat from his body, almost light-headed by his special scent, and she had to fight to avoid going all mushy when she saw that dimple. Even his sardonic smiles displayed that killer dimple!

Watching her, Greg knew no matter how much he teased her, she'd find a way to turn the words back.

He could help easily enough—and eliminate the need for her to call anyone. He knew several men who had talked about settling down, wanting a serious relationship. Maybe even marriage. A quick introduction to Abigail Trent and they could take it from there.

But as he tried to narrow the field of whom he'd want to introduce, he realized he was reluctant to let anyone know the new doctor was looking.

He frowned. He wasn't in the market himself, so why the reluctance to assist her in every way? All he needed to do was make a few phone calls, and wish her all the best.

It was too soon. He'd wait until Elise had helped. Abby had her hair done just as he'd suggested and it looked great. Light and silky, his fingers itched to touch it, feel that softness. But she could use some makeup tips to make the most of her potential—something Elise excelled in. Pam had already done a lot with the dress. For the first time, he wondered what other clothes his sister had sold her.

There was that tantalizing teddy for one.

Would he get a chance to see it? Or would the new man in her life be the only one to see it, take it off her?

He looked away from the shimmering appeal of her eyes. It had been a long time since his thoughts had been so focused on a woman. His one foray into love had proved disastrous and he'd closed his mind to that possibility again.

Sure, he dated occasionally, but his focus stayed on medicine. Michelle had made it abundantly clear to him that he could have one or the other. Medicine was too demanding a mistress to allow a wife to intrude. After only a few months of marriage her demands on his time had been extensive. When he had refused to bow to what he considered unreasonable requests, she'd chosen a different path—as if she wanted to see how many men she could entice. And at the end, she'd flaunted the number.

Their breakup had been messy. Burying his hurt, disappointment and feelings of inadequacy, Greg had devoted his energies to his work. And never forgotten the pain.

Now for the first time in years, he was intrigued with the thought of seeing a woman, spending time with her. Maybe because Abby was a fellow physician, it wasn't quite the same. Or maybe because of the way he felt when she stared up at him through her pretty greenish blue eyes. He didn't ever remember feeling turned on before by a woman's eyes!

Chapter Six

"Oops." She fumbled with her purse when the soft burring sounded. Glancing at her pager, she looked up. "I have to call the hospital. I'll be right back."

He watched her hurry to the foyer for a pay phone. He hoped it was nothing she had to go to the hospital for. Yet if she did, he'd take her. For a moment, if felt odd to have his date be called away. He'd always been the one to be called away in the past.

When she returned, he knew before she spoke she was needed.

"A patient isn't responding well at all to the meds I prescribed. I need to go. The resident wants me to double-check the child."

"I'll take you."

"You don't need to do that. I can get a cab."

"I'll take you, Abigail."

She nodded and gathered her purse and coat. Greg

flagged the waiter and, explaining the situation, quickly settled the check.

In only seconds they were heading for the hospital. The mood of the evening changed. She was all professional dedication now. And any further discussion on dating was out of the question. At least until the child had been stabilized.

Feeling almost abandoned when Abby hurried up to the pediatrics ward, Greg wandered down to the cafeteria. It was practically deserted so late on a Saturday night. He got a cup of coffee and sat near the window. Wryly he wondered if this was how Michelle had felt time after time—pushed to the back, forgotten, as his need to deal with a patient took precedence? For the first time he had a glimmer of understanding about her feelings and views. He had married her and she had been entitled to expect to count on time together with him.

All the more reason to avoid marriage in the future.

Forty minutes later an orderly tapped him on the shoulder.

"Dr. Trent said to find you if I could, sir. She's finished and ready to go home," the older man said genially.

"Thanks." The coffee had long since grown cold, and the thoughts that filled his mind had remained. While Greg didn't believe in involvement, that didn't mean others didn't. He'd introduce Abby to some interested young men and go back to his routine—and a date here and there with a sophisticated woman who knew better than to expect anything beyond a night out on the town.

If Abby ended up getting married, maybe she'd

name her first child after him—if the marriage lasted that long.

With a wry acknowledgment, he conceded he might be growing cynical.

When he stepped off the elevator on the pediatrics floor, one of the nurses smiled at him. ''Dr. Trent is in Room 507,'' she said with a wave toward the hall on the right.

He paused in the doorway, senses alert. Abby was sitting on the side of the bed, brushing the hair from the forehead of her young patient.

''I thought you were finished,'' Greg said.

She looked up. ''I am, just spending a few minutes with Joey. Here's another doctor, Joey. Dr. Hastings.'' She looked up. ''Come meet Joey. He gave us a scare a little while ago, but he's going to be fine. He'll be home before the Giants have their next home game, won't you?''

The little boy smiled trustingly up at Abby and nodded his head vigorously. ''I get to go to some games this summer with my dad and uncle.''

He looked so small in the high hospital bed, almost lost beneath the covers.

''That'll be great, but for now I need you to rest up so you'll be all better real soon. I'll see you tomorrow, Joey,'' Abby promised as she rose and patted his arm. ''And remember, if you want anything, you press this button and Nurse Thompson will be right in, okay?''

''Okay.''

Greg stepped back as she left the room. Turning, they walked to the nurses' station, where Abby made another notation on the boy's chart, then gathered her purse and coat.

''His parents will be here most of the day tomorrow,

so I'll speak with them then. The resident was right to call. I want to make sure he's doing okay."

She glanced up at him. "I guess you're thinking I'm too involved."

"Actually, I was thinking you're a dedicated doctor, and that Joey is lucky he has you as his physician." Greg hesitated a moment, then continued. "And as long as the patient recovers, there's nothing wrong in being involved."

"The key part here is the 'as long as they recover,'" she said.

He nodded.

"We do the best we can."

"And when it's not enough?"

She gazed off into the distance for a moment. "I guess we have to take comfort in the fact we did all we could. But it nearly breaks my heart when someone doesn't respond to treatment."

He found it interesting to see Abby in action. If she treated all of her patients with the care she showed Joey, he suspected every last one of them loved dealing with her.

He glanced at her while they waited for the elevator and was startled to find himself wishing he could reach out to brush an errant lock of hair away from her cheek.

Warning bells went off. The elevator's arrival ended the errant thoughts.

The evening had cooled considerably by the time they stepped outside the hospital, and a light breeze blew from the Bay. Hovering over the Golden Gate, the fog bank was stalled. Later it would sweep across the city, blanketing the hills with its cool dampness.

The evening hadn't gone exactly as he'd planned, but that was the way it was with doctors.

Greg accompanied Abby up to her apartment when they reached her building. Taking her key, he opened her door, reaching around her to flick on the lights.

"Thanks again for bringing me home. It beats coming by myself."

"We didn't get everything settled. I'll ask Elise to lend a hand," he said softly.

"Elise is the model, right?"

He nodded.

"I feel like a family project."

Shrugging, Greg gave in to impulse. Leaning forward, he brushed his lips lightly against hers.

She stepped back in surprise, her eyes wide. He noted the pulse point in her throat, beating rapidly. Greg fought the urge to pull her into his arms. The hot desire that shot through caught him unaware. Her eyes grew wary. Her skin flushed.

It made her all the more attractive. He wanted to put his lips on that pulse, taste her satiny skin, awaken her to the passion that seemed to lurk on the edge.

"This wasn't a date," she said sharply.

That intensity disturbed him.

"Look on it as a way to gain some more experience."

"I'm not sure I need experience in that area. I've been kissed before," she said stiffly.

"Somehow, Abigail Trent, I suspect your kisses have been more the tepid and fraternal type. How long since you were really kissed, dear Doctor?" His hand encircled her neck lightly, drawing her closer. He'd take another kiss before ending the evening. And hope it would be enough.

She dropped her hand against his chest to push him away. But when his lips covered hers, she made no move to push. Heat scorched where her palm rested and, when she flexed her fingers, Greg wondered what it would feel like to have her do that against his bare skin.

Would she let him reciprocate?

Long moments later he pulled back and gazed down at her bemused expression. Her cheeks were fiery, her lips rosy. Her eyes were dreamy. Suddenly he wanted to push her back into the apartment, follow her in and find a bed.

Taking control of emotions that hadn't been that strong in years, he pulled back.

"Abigail, exactly how much experience with men do you have?" His dark eyes studied her as he awaited her response, and his hand at the back of her neck caressed the slender column. He wanted more, but needed to get something clear before the next step.

"That, Dr. Hastings, is none of your business." She spun around and entered the apartment, shutting the door firmly in his face.

Abby leaned against the door, trying to catch her breath. Every cell in her body sizzled. What she could never tell Greg Hastings was that she'd never been kissed like that before! Not by Terry, and never by Jeb. The few dates she'd managed in medical school had been more casual.

She felt stunned at her reaction. Especially in light of what she knew—Greg Hastings was not in any way, shape or form interested in her. She was a project, nothing more.

Waves of shimmering pleasure filled her, a vague,

unfamiliar yearning built deep within while heat seemed to flood her limbs. Floating on a gentle sea of sensation, tingling awareness rippled through. As kissers went, Greg Hastings was a master. Forgotten desire and heat mingled and expanded. Abby never expected to feel like that and especially not with someone she wasn't sure she even liked!

She hoped he didn't suspect how affected she was by a simple kiss.

Simple kiss?

It had been mind-boggling, soul shattering, and she longed to experience it again.

"Dumb, Abby," she said, pushing away from the door and heading for her bedroom.

She might think she wanted more, but she knew it would be totally foolish. He was going to introduce her to eligible men. Any sexual play would mean nothing, not to him. Nor to her. They were professional medical colleagues. He was doing her a favor and she must be extremely cautious to resist reading more into that than there was.

"So how do you explain the kiss?" she asked herself as she prepared for bed.

No answer magically appeared.

When Abby returned home Sunday afternoon after visiting her patients in the hospital, she was surprised to find a stranger sitting on the hallway floor by her door.

The woman rose gracefully and smiled at her. Abby recognized that dimple—it was identical to Greg's.

"You must be Elise," she said.

"I guess you're Dr. Trent."

Abby nodded, reaching to unlock the door. "I didn't

expect you.'' She opened the door and invited Elise Hastings inside.

''I didn't call, took a chance you'd be here. My own fault if I had to wait.'' Elise sauntered in, moving smoothly as if floating. Studying the bright living room, she smiled as she sat on the Queen Anne sofa.

''I've been curious to meet you,'' she said bluntly.

Abby tossed her purse on the table and sat across from Elise. She'd worn slacks and a light top to the hospital. Eyeing Elise's casual clothes, she knew she could never carry off such insouciance. Sighing, she tried to smile brightly.

''I'm not sure why.''

''You're the first woman my brother's been interested in since Michelle-the-witch left him. To find he's enlisting help from both his sisters is totally out of character. I'm dying to know what you and Greg have going.''

Abby stared, fascinated. She didn't know what she wanted to follow up on first, the comment about Greg's wife, or the assumption there was something between them.

Shaking her head, she laughed softly. ''Your brother would die if you suggested to him there was something going on between us. Actually, I think he's a desperate man. Dr. Taylor enlisted his help to escort me to a duty dinner. The hospital fund-raising ball is looming now and he doesn't want to be coerced into escort service again.''

Elise shrugged. ''You don't know my brother well if you think he could be coerced into anything. There's more to it than that.''

Abby considered it. ''Maybe because we are now co-chairs to a committee, he felt incumbent to help me out a bit." It was embarrassing to admit to anyone she needed help, but she didn't know what Greg had already told Elise. Had he made her out as someone needing help before she became too far gone to help?

"Like I said, you don't know Greg very well." Elise shrugged and rose, studying Abby's face. "I can offer some pointers, but I'm not sure what he had in mind. Daily makeup suggestions, or dramatic effects for a night out?"

Abby jumped up, not wishing to feel she was on display.

"Either or both. I have a friend who tried to help for the disastrous dinner."

"Disastrous? How?"

"According to one person, I looked like a tart." Abby tried to keep the hurt from her voice. Coming from one of her best friends, the remark still rankled.

Elise almost smiled. Abby could tell she was too polite to do so, but she wanted to.

"Show me what you've got and we'll go from there," Elise said.

Leading the way to the bathroom, Abby felt self-conscious with a stranger just showing up to help her. Greg could have verified she wanted help before sending his sister.

Or, had Elise jumped the gun because of her curiosity?

Despite her initial trepidation, the afternoon turned out to be fun.

Elise quickly instructed Abby in the best use of the makeup she had, and gave suggestions on other colors to try. Showing her how to highlight her eyes, how to keep the makeup to a minimum during the day, and how to emphasize her best features for evening proved to be enlightening.

During the session, Elise kept her entertained with stories of her modeling career.

After one outrageous tale, Abby laughed. "Are you married? Does your husband mind all that?"

Elise went still, then shook her head. "I'm not married. Don't plan to be."

"Is your brother rubbing off on you?" Abby asked.

"Doesn't have to. I saw what being married did for him. And Pam."

"Pam's married?" Abby hadn't delved into the personal side of Greg's life. Would he mind Elise sharing so much?

"Pam's separated right now. Dave needs to find himself." Her tone convinced Abby that Elise had no sympathy for the man.

"Just up and walked out a few months ago leaving Pam and their daughter, Bethany. She's more tolerant than I would be. I'd have filed for divorce instantly and hit him with everything I could."

"But she didn't?" The Hastings didn't seem to be faring well in the marriage side of things.

"No. She says she'll wait and see what he comes up with. Even after this, she says she loves him and will take him back if that's what he wants. I'd never give the guy the time of day!"

Abby nodded. Didn't she feel the same way about Jeb? She had thought they'd moved closer after Carol died. Now that he'd shown his preference for Sara, she knew she no longer felt the same way about him, or their friendship. She knew now she had never really loved Jeb—not with the love needed to build a marriage.

But if she did love someone that deeply, how would she react if he left and then wanted to come back?

Elise stepped away and studied Abby in the mirror. "That's the best I can do. You didn't need much. When Greg first asked me, I thought you might be a dog and I'd never be able to do a thing."

Abby laughed. "Glad to know you didn't find it so hard."

Elise grinned. "So do we go over to Greg's now and show you off?"

"No way. If he's interested, he can check it out next time he runs into me at the hospital." Interested? His only interest was in making sure she could get another date for the ball and let him off the hook.

Still, as she studied herself in the mirror, it was worth it, to have expert advice. She liked how she looked.

"If you don't have to rush off," Abby said, "I could get us a snack. I have fresh-baked brownies."

"My lucky day. I haven't had a brownie in months. I have to watch what I eat, but usually I do whatever I want on Sundays," Elise said. "I'd love some brownies. And now that we know each other better, and I've talked your ear off, time to reciprocate. Tell me all about the woman behind my brother's request."

Refusing to even consider Greg Hastings had any interest in her beyond their association at the hospital—despite his kiss last night—Abby gave a brief sketch of her background. Soon she and Elise found a mutual interest in books read and their conversation never returned to Elise's brother.

The afternoon passed swiftly. Making plans to get together in another week or so, Abby felt she'd made a friend—though the circumstances of their meeting were odd.

Abby didn't consider herself a vain person, but she had to admit liking to peek into the mirror in the entryway. With her new hairstyle and the subtle makeup Elise had done, she didn't quite look like herself.

With a pang, she wished she could have shared it with Carol and Jeb. It was hard to break the habit of years.

Idly she considered calling Kim. Then another thought came.

Why not call Greg and let him know?

He'd called her old-fashioned because she didn't call men as a rule—not to invite them out on a date in any event. Wouldn't he be surprised to get her call? Not that she was inviting him out on a date. She'd only be calling to let him know any feeling of obligation could safely be discharged. With help from Pam and Elise, she was able to face the Saras of the world, assured she looked her best. She'd never be a blond bombshell, but neither did she really want to be.

She liked her life as it was. It could be enriched by a relationship with a special man, but she'd let fate decide on that. For now, Greg Hastings had provided her the means to move confidently in the social scene.

She didn't have his phone number! A quick check in the phone book showed no Greg Hastings listed. Nor did she have a number for Elise or Pam—except for the boutique. And it definitely would be closed on a Sunday night.

So much for calling Greg Hastings at home.

Wait, had she received a call from anyone else since he'd called her? Maybe, just maybe if she used the feature the phone company offered, she would reach him.

Pressing the button combination as listed in the phone book, she soon heard a phone ringing.

"Hastings."

"Dr. Hastings, I presume?" she said, recognizing his voice instantly.

"Dr. Trent. I didn't expect to hear from you today."

"Are you busy?" Suddenly Abby wondered if he might have invited a woman over for dinner. She had never considered that. "I can call another time, if this isn't good."

"I'm not busy. At least, I was, but can take a break."

"Break from what?"

"Exercising. I don't get enough in during the week, so I do more on the weekends. To what do I owe this call?"

Imagining him in exercise shorts, his body gleaming with moisture, had her heart rate accelerating. The mind was a powerful tool, and Abby was coming to fully understand that. Those butterflies in her stomach had her wishing she had waited. No help for it, though. She'd initiated this call, she had to carry it off.

"I, uh, called to tell you Elise stopped by today."

"She did?" He sounded surprised. "I mentioned you to her, but thought I'd bring her by sometime to introduce you two."

"No need now. Anyway, thanks for all your help."

"Why does this sound like a brush-off?"

"I'm not. I mean, it's not." Confused, she frowned. "How can it be a brush-off? We're not involved."

"More than you may suspect," he murmured.

"Not at all. You offered help. I've accepted. We're square, right?"

"Except for a few introductions."

"I can manage—"

"There's a party some friends are throwing next weekend. Come with me," he said, ignoring her attempt to assure him she was able to manage her own social life!

"Go to a party with you?" For an instant her imagination kicked in. She—wearing a sexy slip of a dress—and Greg, wearing a dark suit, his eyes unable to look away from the vision she presented.

"Don't make it sound so awful. You might even enjoy yourself."

"I thought the last thing you wanted was to be stuck with me again." She blinked the vision away.

"Hmm. That's not quite how I put it."

"The meaning was clear. I'm opting out. No need for you to do anything further. I assure you Dr. Taylor will never approach you again on my behalf."

"That would be too bad."

"What?"

"Come with me to the party. I'll introduce you to a dozen men."

"When would I have time to date a dozen men?"

"You can pick and choose. Saturday at seven."

"I don't know…"

"I do. I'll pick you up at seven. How's the patient?"

"Joey? He's doing really well. If he continues to improve, he'll be going home by Wednesday. The change in meds proved the best thing. Wish I'd done this series first."

"Next time maybe you will. That's how we learn, Abby."

A warm glow spread through her at the intimacy of his tone. Realizing the conversation was not going as she'd planned, she tried to get back on track. But she couldn't remember what she'd been about to say.

"I guess. But it's better when we do it right the first time."

"Always. But we're only human. We're going to make mistakes. The best we can hope for is that any mistake won't prove detrimental to our patients."

"How often do you make mistakes?"

"Not often, thank goodness. But despite our arrogant demeanor, we're just people doing the best we can, right?"

"Yes."

Odd to think philosophically when she'd called to tell him he needn't feel any obligation to assist her further.

"So what did Elise do?"

"Oh, a bit of this and that. I look nice."

There was a pause, then he said, "I always thought you looked nice."

She remembered his comment—quiet and mousy. Did he like mice? "I know the way Kim had me fixed up was too much."

"But you had a reason for it. Has that reason gone?"

"Gone, but not forgotten."

"And that means?"

"I'm not going to try to be something or someone I'm not in the future."

"What you see is what you get, right?"

"Exactly. Though I have to admit, what you see now is better than what you used to see!"

"Then I'll have to pay special attention on Saturday."

When she'd hung up, Abby wondered if she should have resisted the urge to accept his invitation.

Too late. She was committed. It wasn't a date precisely, she would just attend a party with Greg Hastings. She would meet some of his friends, have the opportunity to see the kinds of people he normally associated with.

She would spend hours in his company!

Idly she wondered if there would be dancing. Even colleagues could dance together. The memory of his kiss exploded. Her skin tingled and for a moment her lips imagined they could feel his against them. Closing her eyes she tried to imagine the party, how she'd know just the right thing to say to pique his interest. Then she'd meet all the men he would introduce and be the most sought after woman there. He'd be pushed to the sidelines.

Smiling a bit at her nonsense, she let her imagination sweep Greg back to center stage, demanding she go home with him, since he'd brought her.

And then he'd kiss her good-night—

Abby opened her eyes and jumped up. She had better things to do than fantasize about a slightly cynical doctor who had made it abundantly clear he wanted nothing from her!

Chapter Seven

Wearing another of the new outfits she'd bought from Pam's boutique, Abby took extra pains with dressing Saturday evening. Carefully donning the makeup according to Elise's instructions, she hoped she'd properly expressed her appreciation for Elise's expert guidance.

And Abby hoped to see a spark of interest in some male gaze tonight. Not Greg, she wasn't that foolish. But maybe someone. She wanted to make sure Greg Hastings knew she could attract some male attention.

She was ready when Greg arrived.

"Elise is tagging along," he said as they descended in the empty elevator and headed for his car.

"I'll be glad to see her again. I like her."

"I like her, too, but I didn't expect her to go with us tonight. I had enough of that when we were kids."

Less than fifteen minutes later, Abby, Greg and

Elise walked up to the front door of a stone house in Noe Valley. Lights shone from every window, and the soft sound of music mingled with the chatter of guests floating out on the cool night air.

Elise seemed in a snippy mood. She'd been quiet during the drive and now was complaining about arriving without an escort.

"And what am I?" Greg asked easily.

"You're my brother. That doesn't count."

Elise's expression changed instantly, however, once the door opened. It was as if a light went on inside her. Abby was fascinated. Elise seemed to sparkle and became the epitome of a vivacious, lively and animated young sophisticate. Greeting her hostess with a friendly air kiss near her cheek, she sailed into the thick of things, her disappointment at being escorted by her brother obviously forgotten.

Greg and Abby followed more slowly.

"Greg, I'm so glad to see you!" Angie Jefferies greeted him with an exuberant hug. She was about Greg's age, with light brown hair and a warm, friendly smile. "It's been ages since Hugh's seen you. And far longer for me. He's over there, near the bar."

"You look great, Angie. I'll catch up with Hugh soon. First let me introduce Abigail Trent. Abby, this is Angie Jefferies, an old friend."

Angie laughed. "I prefer long-time friend these days! Hi, Abigail. Welcome. Come with me and I'll introduce you around. Greg, you go talk to Hugh before he gets caught up with someone else." With a friendly motion of her hands she shooed him away and smiled at Abby. Once Greg was out of hearing range, her look became speculative.

"It's been a long time since Greg's brought anyone

to anything. When he called to let us know you were coming, I was so pleased. Have you known him long?''

"Only a few months. We work together at the hospital. We're just friends." Abby felt things were spinning out of control. She had to make that point clear to her hostess. She didn't want Angie to get the wrong idea. Of course one hint to Greg and he'd set everyone straight.

"We've known him since we were all kids. Elise and Pam, too. Come on, I'll introduce you starting with some other long-time friends," Angie said.

The party proved enjoyable, more so than Abby had expected. As the evening progressed, she grew comfortable and gradually lost her feeling of awkwardness and shyness. She'd missed out on a lot of parties because of the studying she needed to do to keep her scholarships through school. Relaxing with Carol and Jeb had been fun, but nothing like this.

From time to time she'd search the room for Greg. Sometimes she'd spot him in the midst of one group or another, other times she couldn't locate him. But even when he caught her eye, he made no move to join her. Not that he needed to, she told herself, ignoring a twinge of disappointment. She was doing fine on her own.

Elise was the center of attention wherever she went. She seemed to have an equal number of women and men friends. At one point Abby decided she wouldn't want that level of attention; she was quite happy with her more quiet nature. But Elise was intriguing to watch.

"Excuse me, I need to speak to Abby," Greg said much later, his arm coming around her waist and deftly cutting her from the small group she was chatting with. He moved them across the crowded room.

"Is something wrong? Did you get called in?" she asked, taken aback yet feeling that fluttery sensation in her midsection again. Couldn't be the wine, she'd nursed one glass all night long.

"Nothing's wrong. I just haven't spent any time with you since we arrived. Are you enjoying yourself?" He slanted a glance at her, his slow smile deepening the dimple.

Abby looked away before she did something stupid. How could that indentation in his cheek wreak such havoc with her senses?

"I'm having a great time. Did you know Margaret Bellingham actually rode in the equestrian event in the last Olympics?"

He nodded. "We went to see her. She did well, except for the last round. It's too bad the other riders gave flawless performances. She just missed a medal."

He headed toward the open French doors leading to the garden. "Want to step outside for a minute? It's hot in here."

Abby nodded, but the warmth she was feeling was directly from Greg's hand at her waist, not the crowd in the room. "I thought you were going to introduce me to a few people tonight," she said as they stepped into the softly illuminated garden. Other couples strolled or sat on the benches around the perimeter.

"Yeah, well there's no one here that you'd like."

"I don't know about that. Elise introduced me to two very nice men, Harry Foster and Derek Williams."

Greg frowned. "Harry's been married three times and Derek is a playboy."

Abby tilted her head as she looked at him, wondering at the tone in his voice. "So?"

"So stay away from them. They're not for you."

A small spurt of anger flared. She pulled away, the better to glare at him. "I can go out with whomever I please. Sharing a committee assignment doesn't give you the right to dictate my private life."

"There's more to it than a committee assignment."

"Oh, your suggestions on how to improve my social life? I thank you, but I think I can manage my own life."

His lips tightened, but he said nothing.

Gradually the serenity of the garden penetrated and Abby felt her sudden anger begin to abate. Just because Greg was dictator in the operating room didn't mean he could order her about! Maybe her telling him so would remind him of that fact.

Before she could say anything further to make her point, however, Elise breezed out into the garden, smiling brightly. "There you two are. I wondered what happened to you. I'm ready to call it a night. How about you?" she said, joining them on the path. "My feet are killing me."

"If you didn't wear such high heels, you wouldn't have that problem," Greg said.

Ignoring him, she turned to Abby. "Did you have fun?"

Abby nodded, her glance sliding toward Greg. "Especially meeting Harry and Derek."

"Derek told me he asked you out next Saturday. We'll have to find something that will dazzle him."

"She doesn't need anything," Greg snapped.

Both women turned to him in surprise. Abby was amazed at the heat that swept through her. Had that been a compliment? From the frown on his face, it was the last thing he had in mind!

Elise laughed and patted her brother on the cheek. "Competition is good for you," she murmured. Smiling brightly at Abby, she nodded toward the house. "Can we go? I'm so tired."

Abby sat in the back of the car with Elise, ignoring Greg's annoyed comment about feeling like a chauffeur. She needed space. Elise chatted vivaciously, recounting all the gossip she'd heard. Most of it meant nothing to Abby, but Greg apparently knew everyone she mentioned.

"Wait here, Elise, I won't be long," Greg ordered when he stopped before Abby's apartment building. He escorted her in silence to her door, using her keys to open it and gently pushing her through. He stepped inside and pushed the door shut. When the door clicked behind him, Abby smiled politely.

"I had a lovely time, Greg. Thank you for inviting me."

"I'm glad you enjoyed yourself. You look pretty in this dress." It came out almost awkwardly.

She blinked, but before she could reply, his lips brushed against hers.

Abby could swear her heart stopped. Had she secretly been wishing for this all night? She felt mesmerized. It wasn't much as kisses went. Would he try again? Please let him try again, she thought.

He did, his mouth teasing hers until she opened for him. It was as if all previous kisses in life had been leading up to this particular one. Abby's emotions soared.

His fingers combed through her soft curls, cradling

her head in his strong palms, holding her in place as his kiss continued to draw a potent response.

One hand trailed down her neck, caressing her, moving across her shoulders and down along her spine.

Abby shivered in anticipation, her hands clutching his shoulders. She felt as if she would float away if she didn't hold on to something solid. And Greg felt very solid.

She reached out to encircle his neck, to press herself against him, delighting in the feel of his firm, muscular frame pressed against her, of his arms around her, of his mouth moving against hers. Mouths opened, tongues touching, bodies pressed together. She was lost to the sensations that swirled through her.

She'd never felt such exquisite excitement before. His fingers slowly stroked and caressed. Her body heated until it felt on fire. Desire threatened to erupt in a caldron of craving need.

Her hands slipped slowly from his shoulders to push aside his jacket and rub lightly against the silk of his shirt. Encircling him, feeling the heat of his own body against her palms, she felt as if she were being drawn deep within him. Leaving her conscious mind behind, Abby felt swept away by the deep pull of attraction she always experienced around Greg.

Greg deepened the kiss, his tongue's forays building the tension and desire within as his hand continued to excite nerve endings until Abby could scarcely stand. She was trembling with reaction and desire and never-before-experienced throbbing need. Clinging to him as if he were her lifeline, she hoped the kiss would last forever.

Hormones, she diagnosed wildly. Chemistry. Why

didn't they teach a course about that in medical school? How to deal with—

The strident buzz of the doorbell shattered the moment.

"Hell!" Greg pulled back and gazed at her, his expression changing.

"Hey, you two, what's going on? Greg, are you taking me home or should I just take a cab?" Elise's voice sounded through the door.

Abby felt momentarily confused. Blinking at the sudden interruption, she tried to think, but she was still too caught up in the spell of his kiss. She could only stand and gaze at Greg with wide-open, startled eyes.

Greg slowly released her.

"I'm coming. I thought I told you to wait in the car," he said as he opened the door.

"It's been twenty minutes. I'm sleepy." Elise looked past him at Abby, her smile sly. "If you want to stay here, I'll take a cab home."

"Don't be silly. Good night, Abby." Greg turned his sister around and pushed her out the door.

"Good night," Abby called faintly. She remained where she stood for several long moments, waiting for her body to cool, for her heart rate to slow, remembering each magical second as she replayed the scene over and over in her mind. She'd never felt so sensuous, so desirable.

Not even with Terry back when she was sixteen and swept away by first love.

She double-checked that the door was locked and headed for her bedroom, her thoughts in a jumble. She wasn't even sure she liked Greg. Why did she have such trouble remembering that?

What had that kiss been about? Why had he even started it?

A thought struck—he didn't think he was helping her gain experience, did he? It sounded so...so cold. Though heaven knows his kisses were anything but cold.

Why did he continue to spend time with her? Why had he offered to help her in the first place? Doubts rose again.

Her thoughts tumbling around in her head, Abby had a hard time falling asleep.

It was late when she awoke. Sundays were lazy days, and Abby had nothing planned, which left her plenty of time to remember last night—the party, the dress, Greg's potent good-night kisses.

The phone rang.

Reaching over, she scooped up the receiver, snuggling back against the pillow lazily. She hoped it wasn't the hospital with an emergency.

"Hello?"

"Did I wake you up?"

"What time is it?" she asked. *And why are you calling me on a Sunday morning?*

"After eleven."

"Then no, you didn't wake me."

"But?"

"Why does there have to be a but?" she asked, wondering what he wanted. Wondering why her heart was racing.

"It was in your voice."

"Very well, then, *but* I am still in bed."

"Wearing that indecent teddy?" His voice dropped intimately, reminding her of dark velvet and brandy and hot summer nights.

And reminding her of the fact he thought she even owned such an sexy garment.

"What else would I wear to bed?" She closed her eyes to listen better.

"One day I want you to wear it for me."

Her eyes flew open. Sitting up, she shivered. The image of her standing before him in that skimpy teddy she'd described was nothing short of erotic. As was the next scene that flashed into her mind, where he slowly peeled it from her shoulders. Good grief, she needed to get control of her wild imagination.

"Abby?"

"We need to change the subject." Her voice was faint. The sooner she distanced herself from this vexing man, the better off she'd be. The last thing she needed was some kind of relationship with the world's most dedicated bachelor.

"Either that, or I'll come over."

"No," she said, surprised at the sudden longing for him to do just that. But she could never carry it off. And one look at her serviceable white cotton gown and he'd mock her for her vain attempts to be seductive. She couldn't even manage bland phone teasing.

"So what are your plans for today?"

"Why?" she asked warily.

"I thought we could take a picnic to Golden Gate Park. It's a beautiful day."

"Why?" she repeated.

"Why not, if you're not doing anything else."

She should say no. She should hang up the phone and think about what to wear when she went to dinner next Saturday night with Derek Williams. She should!

"Okay. I can be ready in a half hour."

"Don't overwhelm me with your enthusiasm. I'll pick you up then." He hung up quickly.

"So I can't change my mind?" she asked as she flung off the covers and rose. He had a habit of hanging up before she was ready. But then, maybe he suspected she'd never be ready.

Half hour later, almost to the minute, Greg knocked on her door. She threw it open. The fluttering in her stomach increased. It was becoming a habit.

"Good morning." The anticipation that rose at the sight of him surprised her.

He wore dark jeans, snug and tight, his strong legs clearly defined. He had on a dark blue shirt that made his brown eyes seem all the richer. He looked tired.

"Ready?"

Still questioning the sanity of the idea, she nodded. "Do I need to bring anything?"

"I have everything in the car."

She picked up her jacket, pleased with her casual manner. She hoped he didn't guess how his presence rocked her. The slim pants she wore were dark green, the better to camouflage grass stains, she'd thought. The pale aqua top made her eyes appear more green than blue. She hoped the day would be warm enough that she could leave her jacket off, but she'd take it just in case. Her hair was loose and flowing around her shoulders.

Abby preceded him to the elevator, glad there was no awkwardness between them after last night's kisses. Apparently Greg had already forgotten the incident. She wondered if she ever would.

It was a beautiful day, though breezy and a bit on the cool side. Frothy whitecaps danced on the Bay, the sky was a deep clear blue, the perfect background for the tall glass and steel of the downtown buildings.

When they reached Golden Gate Park, Greg picked up the picnic basket he'd brought. Slowly they strolled along one of the pathways. The grass was fresh and green after the recent rain, the shrubs and trees washed clean. Flower beds flourished with splashes of red and yellow and blue.

Abby could scarcely contain the bubble of excitement that filled her. They found a deserted grassy area near the arboretum, a dozen yards or so from the path where people walked or skated. Opening the wicker basket, Greg withdrew a small blanket and spread it out.

Abby sat beside him, curiously examining the contents of the picnic basket.

"Where did you get all this, it's fantastic."

"Neiman Marcus. They do picnic lunches."

She looked at him suspiciously. Something wasn't right. The elaborate feast he'd brought was more than a casual picnic in the park. What was going on?

"Hey," he said, shrugging, "it's just lunch."

She nodded, feeling churlish and ungrateful. "You shouldn't have spent so much money."

"If I want to spend money on fancy picnics, that's my choice. Just as yours is to buy sexy lingerie. Are you wearing that silk teddy now?"

She was going to expire from embarrassment. Sitting back on her heels, she kept her gaze firmly on the basket. Heat crept up her cheeks. She remembered every word of their conversation this morning, every image that had danced through her mind. Every sensation that had coursed through her body. How could she have even thought to make up that story about that blasted teddy?

Slowly she shook her head, almost wishing she had bought it. Though she would never be able to wear it, she was sure. And not for Greg. Oh Lord, the mere thought of wearing it for Greg made her dissolve inside.

"A pity." He smiled wickedly at her and lay back on the blanket. "The sun feels good."

She pushed the basket to the side and studied him as he lay with his eyes closed.

"You look tired," she said gently.

"I'm beat. It was a tough week."

"We didn't have to go to that party last night. Though I had a good time," she added hastily. "So what was so tough about this week?"

He opened one eye slightly and looked at her. Closing it again, he said, "Just a full list every day. Next week will be better. I don't have anything scheduled at all for one afternoon. And no dinners."

"Dinners?"

"Uh-huh. I had two last week, both fund-raisers. When you stay out late and then try to work the next day, it's hell. I'm getting too old for that."

She tried to ignore the slight spurt of jealousy that reared up. But it was hard. He'd gone out twice last week to dinners, probably with a beautiful sophisticated woman on his arm. Someone polished and poised and refined. Someone not dumped on him by the department head because she couldn't get a date on her own!

He opened one eye and looked at her.

"What's that frown for?"

"I was just thinking how little I know about you," she said slowly.

"You know the important things. I'm a doctor. I have two sisters, two parents."

"What do they do? Your parents."

"My mother takes care of my dad, mostly. Though she serves on a lot of charity committees. My dad's retired now, but he used to be the chairman of the Trade Commission in the city."

"Why did you ask me here today? What are you getting out of all this?"

"I'll get something. Don't worry." For a moment his voice sounded almost threatening. Abby shivered. Surely she imagined it.

"Like what?" Her throat was dry. Was he expecting some kind of payment?

"Like the company of a charming young doctor, what else?" His voice was lighthearted. She must have imagined an ulterior motive. Greg had never done anything to suggest he wanted something from her—beyond her assistance on the conference committee. And what did she have to offer?

"Surely you'd rather be with someone you've known for years. Someone with whom you have more in common," she said, wondering what the real reason was for his invitation.

"I enjoy doing things with different people, Abby. Don't you?"

"Yes." She smiled shyly at him, almost surprised to realize she was enjoying herself. Trying to relax, she leaned back on her hands and gazed around. Nothing claimed her attention like the man at her side.

He looked so intriguing lying on the blanket, his lashes a dark slash along the top of his cheeks, his hair mussed by the breeze. If she knew him better, would she feel comfortable brushing back his hair, tangling her fingers in its thickness? Her curiosity grew.

She took a deep breath. "Tell me about your marriage," she said daringly.

Greg's eyes snapped opened and he stared at her, astonishment clear in his expression. "Good God, what brought that up?"

She shrugged. "Nothing, I was curious, so I thought I'd ask."

"Michelle and I married right when I got out of school. Things didn't work out the way she wanted, so she made it very clear it was her or medicine. I chose medicine."

"Why did there have to be a choice? Most doctors are married."

"She liked the social scene. And definitely did not like the long hours medicine sometimes required. She wanted a lap dog that she could command to take her hither and yon. When I wouldn't oblige, she left."

"And was she the love of your life?" she asked gently, rubbing her fingers along the seam of her pants, unable to look at him. Almost afraid of his answer.

Greg stared at Abby for a long moment, trying to picture Michelle as he'd remembered her. She'd been tall and blond and trendy. Beyond that, he couldn't remember anything except all the fights at the end.

Abby's shiny blond hair, her unusual eyes, her air of innocence were the antithesis of Michelle despite both of them being blondes. For the first time the bitterness at Michelle's betrayal was missing. He felt nothing thinking about her. His mind was filled with Abby.

"No, she was not the love of my life." He'd

thought so at one time, but now knew better. Or if she had been, maybe he was more shallow than he thought.

"At least I learned something else about you," she murmured, staring across the grass to watch families stroll by with children frolicking on the grass.

"And that is?"

"You're quick to anger. And maybe a bit romantic. Is she the only reason you've sworn to never remarry?"

She looked at him as he sat up, one knee raised, his arm resting on it. "I told you I'm convinced medicine and a family life don't mix."

"Seems lonely."

"Why's that?" His eyes met hers, but the warmth was missing. He studied her coolly.

"No one to share your triumphs with, no one to commiserate with you when you're down."

"I've managed fine all these years."

But there was something in what she said. If he thought about it, he would like some special person to share things with. Someone like his mother, always at home, always putting her husband first. But life didn't always turn out the way he wanted. The price was too high to risk trying again.

"I want more. Maybe it's a woman's thing. But with a new hairstyle, new clothes, I'm ready to venture forth."

"Don't change yourself too much, Abby. You're special just the way you are. Ready to eat?" Greg asked, pulling the basket closer and starting to unpack. He'd meant the day to be carefree. Now he was remembering Michelle and feeling almost sentimental about Abigail Trent!

"I peeked in when you took out the blanket and my mouth has been watering ever since."

Abby moved to help him, her fingers brushing against his once or twice. She refused to look at him, yet he felt the magnetism of his skin to hers, the pull of desire he experienced so easily just by a touch. Her touch.

The lunch he'd brought was special. Pâté and crackers, thinly sliced pheasant and fresh rolls, asparagus in a jell, with a chilled white wine. Rich chocolate truffles for dessert. He'd never known a woman to refuse chocolate.

And for the past few minutes he'd been wondering what she would taste like with wine and chocolate.

Abby had never had such a distinctive meal, and she savored everything. She was full, mellow and replete when she slowly let the last truffle melt in her mouth.

"Mmm, this is wonderful," she said, taking another sip of the wine.

Greg put away the picnic things and pushed the basket to the side of the blanket. Boldly moving next to her, he leaned over to kiss her, his tongue tracing her lips, moving to invade the soft warmth of her mouth.

"Mmm," he said against her lips. "I think this will become a favorite taste."

She smiled and recklessly kissed him back, conscious of the texture of his face, the smoothness of his freshly shaven cheeks, his warm mouth against hers. "Should I always keep a truffle handy, to pop in my mouth in case you want to kiss me again?" she asked whimsically, moving her lips across his mouth as she spoke.

Their breath mingled and fanned across their cheeks. Their lips were sensitized to each other's touch. Greg's hand held the back of Abby's head, his fingers moving against the softness of her hair, holding her face for his kisses, not letting her pull away.

"There's no question I will kiss you again, lady. You can count on it," he said, moving to deepen the kiss, to stop talking and let his lips and tongue convey to her the depth of his attraction.

Abby forgot that they were in a public park, that families and couples and children surrounded them. She gave herself up to the pleasures his special touch brought. Her world spun around, brimming with sensation and sensual awareness. Greg's tongue stroked hers, feeding the heat that extended to the tips of her fingers. His lips moved with hot abandonment against hers, seducing her inhibitions as she responded. She felt wild and free and cherished and desired.

The hoots and jeers from a group of teenagers broke them apart. Abby was breathing hard and her first instinct was to hide her face with the blanket. Scarlet, she looked everywhere but at Greg. He chuckled and waved to the cheeky kids. They laughed and continued on their way, boisterous and full of spirit.

"That's sophistication," she murmured, wishing she could vanish. How could she have let herself be so caught up in his embrace in a public park? She wanted to sink beneath the blanket and hide.

He nodded. "Good thing they interrupted us, I'd forgotten where we were."

So she wasn't the only one to get caught up in their kiss. Mollified slightly, she smiled and looked bravely around, still unwilling to meet his eyes. How best to handle this?

"Want to go for a walk?" she asked, anxious to escape the scene. How many people had watched them?

"Yeah, sure. We can work off some of that lunch. Besides, it's too early to call it a day."

Chapter Eight

The sun had warmed the afternoon, the air mild and scented with the fresh-cut grass. Neither needed their jackets, so Abby carried them while Greg carried the basket.

"Where did you grow up, Abby?" Greg asked as they walked along the wide beaten path.

"On a ranch up near Yreka. My dad raises cattle. We took a lot of picnics, only we called them working lunches. We'd eat out on the range surrounded by new calves and stoic cattle." She smiled at the memories. "Sometimes the calves would come up and want to see what we were eating. But usually we were ignored."

"Pretty country, Northern California."

"Yes, but quiet and slow. I like living here in the city."

"Definitely more to do."

"I think so. And I felt there'd be more scope here for a doctor. I can make a bigger difference," she said slowly.

"Yet you want to get married. Won't that prove difficult if you're still working?"

"*If* I'm still working? Greg, I plan to work as a doctor all my life. Getting married won't change that. When you were married you still worked, right?"

"What if you became a mother?"

"If you were a father, you'd still work, wouldn't you?"

"It's not the same thing."

"Excuse me, you're telling me you think a woman should stay at home and raise children and do nothing else?"

"My mother did."

"So did mine, because it was what she wanted. I applaud her for it. But it is not what I want. I want a husband and family, but I want my career, as well. Good grief, I've trained for years to become a doctor. I wouldn't give it up just because I got married or had a baby."

"And you think you can handle both?"

"I think my husband will be supportive of me and together we will both handle careers and our family," she said firmly.

"Then we better get working to find this paragon of a husband you want. Some man who will let you walk all over him until he ends up staying at home with the babies. I wouldn't put up with it," he growled.

"That sounds positively Neanderthal. Most women work outside the home today. And have lovely families! Fortunately not everyone thinks like you do!"

"Too bad, maybe things would be better if they did."

"I doubt it. I'm sorry your marriage didn't work out, but I doubt it had much to do with medicine. I expect it had to do with you and Michelle as people."

"Let's get out of here. This isn't working."

"Just because I don't agree with you?" she asked.

"Not just that. There's no point in dragging things out. You and I obviously come from two very different areas on the spectrum. You live in your rosy-colored world and I live in reality. The fact is doctors make lousy spouses. But you'll have to find that out for yourself when you finally grow up, won't you?"

Hurt at his words, Abby raised her chin. What a disastrous way to end the date.

Not date!

"Fine. In fact, you can just let me know where I can pick up a cab and we won't *drag anything out any longer!*"

He glared at her. "I brought you, I'll take you home."

She stopped in the path, hands on hips and glared back, anger sweeping away the hurt. "I can manage fine on my own."

"No one ever said you couldn't, Dr. Trent! But I'll still take you home."

Seething in silence the entire ride, Abby tried to figure out what had changed so radically. Obviously talking about his marriage was a topic to be avoided at all costs!

But his behavior only strengthened her belief in his ruthlessness. They could have changed the subject and continued.

When he reached her apartment, she opened the door before the car came to a full stop.

"Lunch was delicious, the company less than desirable. I am all grown-up, Dr. Hastings. Why don't you try it yourself?"

Slamming the car door, she stormed into the apartment lobby, still so angry she could scream!

No one had forced him to invite her to the picnic. No one forced him to spend any time with her at all. She was furious with herself that she had acquiesced to Dr. Taylor's edict to have Greg escort her to that ill-fated dinner. She should have said no, stayed at home and locked the door!

She caught herself in time to keep from slamming her own door. No need to disturb the neighbors because of Greg Hastings.

And she need never see the man again—except in the course of their duties. Which would mean practically never.

Soon she'd meet someone she could grow to love and it wouldn't be some scarred doctor who was not into marriage and, if he ever did marry, thought a woman's place was in the home.

Not that her track record was so great, she thought dismally, sinking onto the sofa and gazing off into space. First Terry, then Jeb. Now Greg.

Not that she had any feelings for the man. He was the last man to become involved with.

But the picnic had been fun at the beginning. And the party last night had been different and enjoyable.

Jumping up, she strode purposefully into her bedroom. She'd plan exactly what to wear to make Derek glad he asked her out. And she'd have a fabulous time with him. And with Harry if he asked her out.

Greg Hastings could eat his heart out!

Abby spent most of the week staying strictly in the pediatrics wing. There was a call from Rose about a committee issue. Abby instructed her nurse-cum-secretary to respond rather than return the call herself.

Wednesday afternoon she'd become used to avoiding any place Dr. Hastings could be found. And just in case the hospital gossip was running rampant again, she took time to stop and chat with other doctors and some of the nurses to diffuse any speculation of the situation between her and the surgeon.

"Hey, Abigail, you leaving on time tonight?" Mike Adams, one of the young interns assigned to pediatrics, leaned casually against her office door frame. He was tall, blond and fun loving. A couple of years younger than Abby, he never seemed to take himself or anyone else seriously. The direct antithesis of Greg Hastings.

Abby nodded. "Is there a problem?"

"No. I just wondered—how about dinner? I know a nifty Italian place not too far from here. Their marinara sauce is out of this world."

The last thing Abby expected was an invitation to dinner! Mike had always been friendly, teasing her and making her laugh. He'd even shared coffee with her a few times when they'd discussed patients. He was easy to be around.

She stared at him a full minute before she answered. Why was he asking her out?

What was her choice for the evening? Go home to an empty apartment and memories that wouldn't leave her alone?

"That sounds like fun," she said slowly, trying to smile. "I should be finished by six."

"I'll swing by here and pick you up. We'll go straight from work and get a jump on the dinner crowd. We can walk if the weather stays nice."

"Okay. See you then." She watched him walk away, wondering why she didn't feel that fluttering sensation when in Mike's presence. He was just as good-looking in his way as Greg Hastings was. Actually more fun to be around. She didn't feel she had to watch herself with him. Of course he treated everything in a lighthearted manner, but she never doubted his dedication. Any more than she doubted Greg's.

Frowning, she drew another patient's file from the stack and opened it. She couldn't think about Greg Hastings!

The rest of the afternoon flew by. By six, Abby had second thoughts about dinner. She was tired and still feeling discouraged and uncertain of her own ability to recognize the good guys when she saw them. Knowing she'd be poor company, she considered asking Mike for a rain check. But when he arrived at her desk with a bright bouquet of daisies, her spirits lifted. She refused to disappoint him.

"I'll be ready in two minutes. Thanks for the flowers, they'll brighten the place." She quickly filled a glass to hold the flowers and made a last-minute check on her makeup. Replenishing her lipstick, she was pleased at the way her hair looked, even after a full and hectic day.

"Ready?" His appreciative glance swept her from head to toe, and came right back up to her eyes. His smile was friendly, nothing more.

"Yes. I like the flowers."

"You look like a daisy kind of girl. Wholesome and fresh," he said easily as they descended the elevator.

"Oh, great, just what a woman wants to hear. Wholesome—yuck!"

He laughed and gently bumped his shoulder to hers. "Would you rather everyone saw you as some slinky siren?"

"Yes, actually, I would," she teased back. "At least during non-business hours."

She hesitated only a second when she recognized the tall dark man leaning against the admitting desk watching the elevators. She had not expected to see Greg. Who was he waiting for? She glanced up at Mike, hoping she could make her expression adoring. Greg needn't think just because he wasn't interested in marriage all men were the same.

Tucking her hand in Mike's arm, she leaned into him slightly. "How far away is the restaurant?" She hoped the rapid pounding of her heart wasn't evident.

"Not far, a ten-minute walk." Mike smiled down at her easily and covered her hand with his. "I love Italian food. Think I could eat it every day."

"Abby!" Greg called, straightening from the desk.

She looked up, as if surprised. Nodding once, she turned away, facing forward.

"The famous Dr. Hastings. A friend of yours?" Mike asked softly, hesitating as he looked at the dark man glaring at them from across the lobby.

"Just another colleague. He and I are on the conference committee." She shrugged, tugging slightly on his arm. "I'm glad we're walking. The fresh air will feel good."

Mike gave Greg a curious glance but continued on their way. By the time they reached the sidewalk, he began recounting a funny incident that had occurred during his shift and Abby forced herself to pay attention, laughing at all the right places.

Even as she tried to listen to Mike her attention was focused on Greg. What was he doing? Had he given up, or was he still watching her? It was all she could do to refrain from turning around.

Abby tried to be a good dinner companion, but found it hard. She couldn't help comparing Mike with Greg. Mike was funny and nice but didn't hold the attraction that Greg held.

He did his best to keep her entertained, but twice he had asked her if anything was wrong. She denied it and he didn't seem particularly worried that she lapsed off. He'd gently tease her and repeat what he'd said. Abby was grateful he was so undemanding. But then he was just looking for a friend to eat dinner with.

"How about we take in a show this Saturday night?" Mike asked as coffee was being poured.

"Can't, I already have a date."

"Okay, how about I switch with Steve on Friday night and we go out then."

She studied him. "Why?"

"I like your company."

She liked his. Tonight's dinner had been entertaining and fun. Granted, bells hadn't gone off, but then they never had. That was just something she'd read in books.

Greg's image rose. Firmly relegating it to the back of her mind, she smiled. "Okay. Italian again?" she asked. At least she wouldn't be home again next Friday night if Greg stopped by. For a moment she wondered if she was doing the right thing. Her heart was not fully in it, but she had to make a start somewhere.

"How about Chinese next time. Would that suit?"

The way he moved his rangy body reminded her for a second of Elise. Was everything going to remind her of Greg or his family in the near future?

"Sounds delicious, what time?"

"I'll pick you up at seven. That'll give you a chance to get home and change. Dress casually, I want to unwind, not have to fight the dressy scene."

At least Mike seemed genuinely interested in friendship, never dropping innuendos into his conversation, never touching her beyond a casual brush.

When dinner ended, they walked back to the hospital to pick up their cars. He insisted on following her to her apartment.

"I want to make sure you get home safely, and besides, I need to know where to pick you up Friday, right?"

"I could give you directions."

"Yeah, but the evening is early and I don't have anything else to do. If I follow you home, you might ask me up for coffee."

"Consider yourself invited—but just for one cup. The evening is young, but I need to catch up on my sleep."

She parked on the street near the corner and waited while Mike found a space a block away and began walking toward her. When he was close enough, he began speaking, "Know what I like about you?"

"That I never yell like Dr. Hastings is known to do?" she replied, growing a little tense. She didn't want the evening to turn romantic.

"No, you remind me of my sister."

That was definitely not romantic. Abby relaxed.

"Is there a compliment somewhere in there?" she

asked as she turned and fell into step. It wasn't far to the front door of the apartment building.

He smiled and nodded. ''I'm comfortable around you. I don't have to maintain my image. I can just enjoy the evening with a pretty woman without expecting her to want more from me than that. Right?''

''What more would someone expect?''

''Fascinating conversation from a doctor,'' he said sarcastically.

She had enjoyed the evening. It reminded her of the many nights she and Carol and Jeb had gone to dinner somewhere and ended up drinking endless cups of coffee and discussing everything under the sun.

She'd missed that.

''So we'll be friends,'' she said firmly. ''I think I'd like that.''

He smiled at her and nodded, toying with her hair as it curled around his finger. ''Don't sound so surprised. Some women like spending time with me,'' he teased.

She smiled. ''I didn't mean to sound surprised.''

''Then don't be surprised when I kiss you, either.'' At her look he grinned. ''I kiss my sister, too.''

His lips covered hers lightly. There were none of the explosive sensations she experienced when Greg kissed her. It was like kissing her cousin or her father.

''Did you throw over my brother for him?'' asked a sarcastic voice.

Abby jerked back and spun around. Elise was leaning against the fender of a car, her eyes darting between Abby and Mike. She was dressed in skintight black jeans and a black jersey top that clung to her like a second skin. Her dark hair was drawn back and her makeup was dramatic. Her eyes narrowed as she waited for Abby to respond, chilling in their coolness.

"Elise! I didn't expect to see you."

"Obviously not." She pushed herself upright and sauntered up to Abby, her eyes bright with interest in Mike.

"Who's your friend?" she asked insolently.

"Dr. Mike Adams, meet Elise Hastings. Mike works at Merrimac General with me."

"I see you stick with doctors," Elise said.

Mike seemed amused, avidly watching the interplay between the two very different women.

"I hear you're mad at my brother." Elise's attention turned to Abby.

"No." Anger suggested a stronger emotion than she'd admit to. "Annoyed, maybe."

Elise shrugged casually, elegantly. "He says mad. I came to get the lowdown."

"Would your brother be the illustrious Dr. Hastings of Merrimac General?" Mike asked.

"Yes."

"I didn't throw him over. We are on that committee together, nothing more," Abby snapped, opening the outside door to the apartment building.

"Are you going to invite me up, Abby?" Elise asked impatiently.

"She's already invited me for coffee," Mike interposed smoothly.

Feeling as if the situation were totally out of control, Abby pushed open the door. "Both of you can come up for one cup," she said ungraciously. Elise was the last person she had expected to see tonight.

"Did you really come here because of Greg?" Abby asked when Elise followed her into the small kitchen a few minutes later. Mike was right behind her, stopping to lean against the doorjamb.

"No, I came to see what you're wearing for your date with Derek." With a dark glance at Mike, she turned her back on him. "But when I saw your date, I had to ask."

"I can date whomever I wish." Hadn't she made that plain to Greg when he challenged the idea of her going out with Derek.

"Hey, I never said you couldn't." She began to smile. "Did someone else tell you that?"

"I heard Derek is a playboy and Harry has been married three times."

"Who are Derek and Harry?" Mike asked.

Elise shrugged and sank onto one of the chairs that encircled the small table. "Friends of mine I introduced to Abby."

"Abby?" He raised an eyebrow and looked at her.

She hardly noticed Greg calling her that anymore. But she wasn't sure she wanted just everyone calling her Abby.

"Now isn't that interesting," Elise mused, ignoring Mike. "Why would he care who you see?"

"Who?" Mike asked.

"Do you mind?" Elise said, glaring at him again. "I'm trying to have a conversation with Abby."

"I'm trying to figure out what you're talking about," he replied, his smile denoting the amusement he found in the situation.

Abby kept busy getting down cups and saucers, taking the cream from the refrigerator and finding the sugar bowl.

"Isn't what interesting?" Abby asked.

"That Greg's putting in his two cents about who you see."

"I don't find that interesting, I find it obnoxiously interfering."

"Whew, but how do you really feel?"

Abby frowned at Elise. "I feel like dropping the subject. Do you want a brownie?"

"No. I mean yes, but today's not Sunday, so I'll pass."

"Elise is a model," Abby explained to Mike, trying to maintain a semblance of normality in a situation that was fast turning into a farce.

How could she get rid of her guests? She didn't want to talk about the situation with Greg. She didn't like the insinuations Elise was making about her relationship with her brother. There was no relationship.

And she sure didn't want to give Mike any food for thought about it. The last thing she needed was more grist for the rumor mill.

The phone rang.

Saved by the bell. She excused herself from her guests and hurried into the living room to answer. Maybe her unwanted guests would take the hint and leave.

"Abigail."

It was Greg. Good grief, was there no getting away from the man?

Her heart lurched in her chest, her breath caught. Just hearing his voice warmed her to her toes. She took a deep breath. Time to take control somewhere.

"I can't talk now, I have company."

"Where have you been?"

"I don't have time to talk," she repeated. "Mike is still here."

"Has he kissed you?"

"That's the most outrageous question I've been asked. Are you standing in for my father at this late stage?"

"What do you mean?

"My dad didn't cross-examine me when I was a teenager. I sure don't answer to that now. I've got to go."

"Who is it?" Elise asked from the kitchen doorway.

"Your brother," Abby snapped.

"Is Elise there?" Greg asked.

"Yes, it's a regular party over here. Good night." She hung up the phone and placed her hands on her hips, aware of tension in the air that hadn't been there before.

"I'll come by another time, Abby, when we can talk uninterrupted," Elise said, heading for the door, her head held high.

"I'll give you a ride home," Mike said easily, his eyes dancing in amusement. Abby wondered what had gone on while she'd been on the phone.

Elise started to refuse, then shrugged. "Why not, I've never spent much time with a doctor before, except Greg. Can I get a free consultation?"

Mike kissed Abby again when she saw them both to her door, his eyes laughing down into hers. "Keeping up the image," he whispered before he followed Elise's ramrod-straight back from the apartment.

If she lived to be a thousand, Abby knew she'd never understand men!

Chapter Nine

Abby had a few free minutes Thursday morning—a minor miracle these days. She jotted down the notes from her last patient and tossed the folder in the out basket. Leaning back against her chair, she rubbed her forehead. The nagging tension that had been present since last night wasn't going away. How could a simple dinner with a friend have produced such turmoil?

She wanted to know why Elise had stopped by last night. And why she'd dashed away so quickly. Abby called Pam's boutique, but Pam wasn't in and the salesclerk refused to give out Elise's phone number.

Which was prudent, she knew, but aggravating when she wanted it. Who knew when she'd have another lull? Reluctantly she dialed Greg's extension.

Rose answered.

When she heard Abby's request, she hesitated. ''I

don't know, I'd have to check with Greg first,'' she said.

"Never mind," Abby said quickly. "I'll call her from home tonight. It's just that I had a few minutes free. Thanks anyway." She hung up before Rose could suggest waiting while she asked Greg.

She'd take her few minutes and go get a cup of coffee, then plunge back into her appointments.

When Abby returned to her office ten minutes later, she almost spilled her coffee when she saw Greg lounging against the side of her desk, leafing through one of the medical journals she kept meaning to read.

He looked up when she stopped, his eyes narrowing.

"Rose said you wanted Elise's number."

Abby took a deep breath, wondering how she could go from calm, focused physician one minute to fluttering feminine awareness and desire the next.

Desire?

Squashing any thoughts along those lines, she took a deep breath and nodded, stepping into her office. She rounded the desk and sat down quickly before her knees gave way.

"I had some time between appointments and thought I'd call her. We, er, didn't get to visit that much last night."

"I guess not, with her crashing your date."

The odd note in his voice made her curious. She looked up. "It wasn't precisely a date, we just went to dinner together."

"Next you'll tell me you two are just good friends."

There was something odd about his tone. She couldn't place it, however. Slowly she shrugged.

"I don't know if I'd call us good friends. We do work together."

"Dating a fellow physician could be dangerous."

Dating Greg Hastings could be dangerous. Seeing Mike Adams was a walk in the park.

She sipped her coffee, more for something to do than that she still wanted it. Her peaceful break had ended.

"Do we scratch our plan?" Greg asked, leaning forward enough that Abby felt as if the air had been sucked out of the room. She tried to inch away without appearing obvious, but she was afraid he knew her every thought.

"Plan?"

"To find you a date for the hospital ball. Has Mike asked you?"

She stiffened. "I've told you I can manage that part just fine. And no, he didn't ask me."

"You could ask him," he said silkily.

Abby stood just as her nurse stepped to the door.

"Your next patient is in room three," Margaret said, eyeing Greg with a puzzled air.

"Thank you, Margaret, I'll be right there." Abby waited until the nurse had left before facing him. "I think whoever I go with will be my business. If you want to give me Elise's number, please do, otherwise—I have a patient to see."

He leaned over, appropriating her pen and notepad, and dashed off the seven-digit number. Scarcely pausing, he then added another number and an address.

"My number and address if you need it," he said.

She waited for him to leave, but he made no move to do so, tossing the pen and pad back onto the desk and looking at her.

"Are you still seeing Derek on Saturday?"

She nodded. Did she imagine the tension rising in the room?

"I don't think you should."

"Thank you for your opinion, Doctor. When I want it, I'll ask for it."

He studied her for a moment, shrugged and rose. Just before leaving the office, he glanced back at her. "Have breakfast with me Sunday? I want to discuss another suggestion regarding the conference."

"Breakfast on Sunday? Can't we meet next week?"

"We could, but my schedule is hectic and I wanted to update the staff at the meeting on Tuesday. Do you have other plans for breakfast?"

She glared at him. "No, I don't. Fine, we'll discuss the conference on Sunday. What time?"

"Early?"

Exasperated, she snapped, "How about five in the morning, or is that too early for you?"

"I'll pick you up at eight." That amusement was back in his eyes.

Abby's heart raced. How could she let him manipulate her like that?

Unless, of course, she secretly wanted to have breakfast with him?

"Eight." She took another big swallow of her coffee and headed for examining room three. Greg watched her until she was almost at the door. Was he planning to force her to squeeze by?

"Was there something else?" she asked, stopping just inches away. Inhaling the scent of his aftershave when she took a breath, she tried to quell the sensations that filled her. Images of that kiss flooded. For a moment she wondered if he'd kiss her again.

But not in the hospital. Not in an open doorway to the hallway dozens of staff members used.

When his hand came up, she thought for an instant she was wrong, he would kiss her wherever he wanted and to hell with what others thought.

She almost swayed toward him.

His fingers brushed against her cheek and moved to her ear—tucking back an errant strand of hair.

Abby blinked, aware of the darkness of his eyes, the sensations tumbling around that had her forgetting where she was going and why.

"Until Sunday morning, then," he said softly, intimately. "Enjoy your date."

Smooth, Greg thought, annoyed with himself, as he watched her hurry down the corridor. Jamming his hands into his pockets, he headed in the other direction, toward the elevators. Reaching the stairwell door, he changed direction and took the stairs. He needed something to get rid of this restless energy.

He had a bone to pick with Elise. How could she set Abby up with Derek Williams? The man was light-years ahead of Abby in the dating scene. He'd eat her alive and she wouldn't even know what hit her.

But would she take his advice and cancel? No, she was so determined to prove to him she could get her own dates, she didn't listen to reason.

And that would be? his conscience asked.

Frowning at the trend of his thoughts, he reached the floor where his office was located. He had another consultation soon. But his thoughts weren't with the new patient, but with Abby and Derek. Damn the man, if he hurt her, he'd answer to him!

He nodded at Rose as he passed by, closing the door to his office behind him.

Abby's cheek had been so soft, her hair so silky. His fingertips could still feel her. And it had been touch-and-go for a minute. He'd wanted to sweep her into his arms and kiss her again. Feel the burgeoning passion that fascinated him. Feel her warmth engulf him, her soft sounds that delighted. She was so open when she showed her delight with what happened when they kissed.

Almost groaning, he sat at his desk, annoyed he hadn't kept his hands to himself, and couldn't better keep his imagination under control.

Time to get her out of his mind, to focus on medicine and his patients, he thought. He wasn't in the running for any kind of long-term relationship, so why wouldn't he wish the best for her? Introduce her to a few friends. He could dance with her at her wedding.

He frowned, pulling forward the patient's file and trying to forget the disquieting thought dancing with her brought.

But the nagging feeling stayed with him all day. He didn't want Abby going out with anyone else. He didn't want to picture anyone else kissing her, holding her, caressing her.

How low could a man get? He didn't want her, but neither did he want anyone else to have her.

As was their habit every other Saturday, Kim and Abby did their grocery shopping together. While taking advantage of specials, picking their way through the meat department sales, and the wide variety of vegetables, Kim questioned Abby about her date with Mike the previous evening.

"It was nothing but a dinner with a friend," Abby said, trying to deflect her friend's curiosity.

"Are you seeing him again?"

"Umm, maybe next Friday night."

"But that's nothing special?" Kim teased.

"No, it's not." And it wasn't. The meal had been pleasant, but if Mike showed any signs of wanting more from her than a friend to eat with occasionally, she'd stop seeing him.

Kim was telling Abby about a new recipe for corn-bread she'd tried when they stepped off the elevator on their floor.

Once again Elise was in the hallway sitting on the floor beside Abby's door.

"I'm going to have to get a bench," Abby said as she unlocked the door, balancing bags of groceries.

Elise reached out and took one. "I could have called, but I thought you'd be home. What time do you get up to go shopping so early?"

"We like to beat the crowd." Abby quickly made introductions. "Come back when you've put away the groceries," she suggested to Kim.

Elise watched Kim continue down the hall before following Abby into her apartment.

"She's the one who dolled you up for that banquet, isn't she?" Elise asked, when she placed the bag on the counter.

Abby nodded, unpacking.

"She's got the style for flamboyance. You don't."

"Thanks a bunch," Abby murmured, opening the refrigerator and stashing the milk and eggs.

Elise hopped up on the counter and watched her. "Do you want to be flamboyant?"

Abby shook her head, "Not really. Mostly I like who I am. But—"

The old feelings of inadequacy flooded. Terry's scathing comments, her lack of experience and the rejection of Jeb all cumulated to make her insecure and uncertain in the social scene. As a physician, she knew she was good. As a woman, she still felt the failure Terry had made her out to be.

Logically she knew it hadn't been her. At least not all her. But—emotionally it was a different story.

"Abigail?"

She looked at Elise and tried to smile, hoping she'd given nothing away. "Kim is certainly at ease with men, flirting with them like it's a huge game. Even with the bag boys at the supermarket, and they're teenagers. It's as if she practices on any male in the vicinity."

"Some women like to do that."

"And are so good at it."

"Takes practice. Do you want to be good at it?"

"Better than I am, maybe."

"Now isn't that interesting," Elise drawled. "Whom do you wish to flirt with, dear Doctor?"

Abby threw the empty egg carton at her and laughed. "No one!" Never in a million years would she admit to the slightest urge to test her ability with Greg Hastings—especially with his sister!

Elise caught the carton and smiled slyly, her eyes assessing. "Practice tonight with Derek. That's why I stopped by—to see what you're planning to wear and all. Where are you going?"

"Dinner at some place on Union Street."

"Balcomb's, I bet. They have dancing there. Derek

loves to hold women against him. He plain loves women.''

''Your brother isn't too wild about him.''

''And you would know that because?''

''Because he's told me so several times. Loud and clear. He thinks I'm in over my head.'' Abby put the last of the canned goods in the cupboard and shut the door.

''He could have asked you out for tonight. If he wants you to avoid other men, he'd better step up the pace.''

''For heaven's sake, Elise, there is nothing going on between your brother and me!''

''Do you want there to be?'' Elise asked irrepressibly.

''No!'' Abby carefully folded the paper bags and slid them beside the refrigerator, wishing she had a moment to herself. Time to change the subject.

''How did you and Mike fare on the way home the other night?''

''What do you mean?'' Elise asked sharply.

Abby looked at her in surprise. Now Elise was concentrating on flattening the egg carton.

''The tension between the two of you, when you left, was so thick I could have cut it with a knife. Since I saw him walking around on Thursday, I figured he'd made it through unscathed.''

''He's not my type.''

''What's your type?''

''Footloose and fancy-free, just like me. I'm not into long-term relationships.''

''What is it with your family that none of you want to commit?''

"Pam did, and look where it got her. Greg did a long time ago, and got burned. Why should I try it?"

"Aren't your parents happy?"

Elise shrugged. "I think they are, but who knows what really goes on. Maybe my mother is too afraid to go out on her own."

"Good grief, you're cynical."

"And you're not. You look at life through rose-colored glasses, I bet. You must scare Greg half to death."

"What?"

"He's got the hots for you, I can tell. But you're nothing like the women he normally sees. Or started seeing after Michelle."

"He's not seeing me."

"Maybe that's the problem."

"What problem?"

"He's as grouchy as a bear. Called me up to ask what I thought I was doing siccing Derek on you."

Kim knocked and Abby dashed to the door, relieved to get that awkward conversation interrupted.

Kim had the knack of making friends instantly. Soon she and Elise were chatting away like old acquaintances. Abby was relieved that the conversation stayed firmly away from Greg Hastings!

A half hour later Pam showed up.

"I brought you something," she said, holding up a plastic-wrapped dress. "I heard from Elise you were going out with Derek tonight. So I picked out a super dress. He always takes his dates to wonderful places."

"Come in. Elise is here and my friend Kim."

The afternoon sped by. For the first time since Carol's death, Abby felt close to other women. Had Carol not died, Abby suspected she would have loved her new friends, as well. Elise's edge of cynicism was amusing. Pam hid the fact she was longing for her husband, and did her best to soften Elise's cynical remarks. Kim laughed and countered with outrageous comments that had them all laughing.

Abby would never forget her best friend, or cease regretting her death at such an early age. But today proved she could move on, could enjoy life to the fullest. Maybe because of Carol's early death, she knew she should cherish every moment.

And she planned to do just that—every minute—as a tribute to her friend, who would never again be able to do so.

Dinner with Derek, however, didn't prove to be the wonderful event she'd hoped for. She could tell he was used to being the center of attention. His conversation was polished and amusing, but not real. Half of what he said was for effect. While entertained, she felt vaguely cheated. Didn't he care enough to be honest about who he was? What he thought?

When she was paged, she could tell he was annoyed.

Fortunately she handled the matter on the phone in a few moments. Returning to their table, however, she couldn't help but wonder how he would react if she'd been called in like she had been with Greg.

For one tantalizing moment, she considered making up an emergency just to end the evening. But her innate sense of fairness won out. Derek had invited her for dinner and dancing, she'd accepted. She had to see the evening to the end.

If Greg thought she'd be swept off her feet by Derek, he'd been sadly mistaken. If anything, Derek reminded her of Terry—wildly popular, considering himself God's gift to women.

And shallow and self-centered.

She refused to invite him in for coffee when he hinted broadly as he walked her to her door. She turned her face at the last moment so his good-night kiss landed on her cheek.

With the door firmly shut behind her, she breathed a sigh of relief. If dating meant spending hours with men who bored her silly, she'd give it up before starting.

She didn't need to date, just to find someone to take her to the hospital's ball. After that, she could do whatever she wanted. But she would never let Greg Hastings think she couldn't get a date!

Promptly at eight the next morning the doorbell rang. Abby had been ready for ten minutes. She had a folder with notes she'd taken about the conference, and stashed it in the large purse she slung over one shoulder.

The tailored slacks and soft white silk top were suitable for a business breakfast, she thought, opening the door. All thoughts of business fled the instant she saw Greg. He looked fantastic!

Worn jeans hugged his long legs. The pullover shirt lovingly delineated every muscle in his chest and shoulders. The wind-tossed hair had her longing to push it back into some semblance of order. And his dark eyes mesmerized as he slowly smiled.

The dimple appeared and her heart turned to mush.

Try for some control, she told herself, but the thought faded as her overactive imagination began to wonder if he'd kiss her again. Just the brief thought had her breasts tightening in longing, her lips parting as if readying themselves for his.

Blast it! She was becoming fixated on his kisses.

"Ready?" That husky tone would sound wonderful whispered in a woman's ear late at night—in bed.

Taking a deep breath, Abby dropped her purse. Clattering, it broke her gaze and she glanced down to see the contents spilled hither and yon.

Greg stooped to begin picking up the few items within reach. She scrambled for the rest, embarrassed to have him see how much junk she carried.

"Do you need that? Just bring your keys," he suggested, handing her the purse.

"It has the notes from the conference committee in it," she mumbled, afraid to meet his gaze again in case she did something even more stupid, like throw herself into his arms and ask for a kiss!

Last night has been totally different. Why couldn't she feel the same kind of indifference toward Greg she'd felt for Derek?

"You can remember anything we discuss." He took the purse and held it open. "Just get your key."

She could argue. She could say she didn't want to follow his orders, but she merely complied, pulling out her house keys and her pager. Clipping the small device on her waistband, she tucked the keys into her pocket.

All the way down in the elevator, Abby waited for Greg to ask her about her evening with Derek. But, except for a casual comment about the weather, he remained silent. When she risked a glance, he seemed miles away.

Feeling a bit piqued, she also kept silent, but inside tension began to build. Didn't he care anymore that she'd spent the evening with Derek Williams, lady killer par excellence?

Greg opened the passenger door for her and made sure she was seated before closing it. Watching him round the hood, Abby was again struck by the intense feelings she always seemed to experience around him. Foolish daydreams clamored for release. She clamped down on them firmly.

When he started the engine, she smiled brightly, hoping her expression didn't look as forced as it felt.

"So where are we going?"

"To a bakery not far from here. They have the best Danish pastries, croissants, doughnuts and bagels."

"Are we supposed to eat it all?" she asked mildly. The first bit of enthusiasm she'd seen today and it was about food. What about her hair, which she'd gotten up extra early to do? He hadn't even noticed the makeup she'd applied so skillfully thanks to Elise's help.

He glanced at her, then looked back to the road. "No, but you'll have a choice. And they have the best coffee this side of Seattle."

The bakery was crowded when they squeezed their way inside the door. The line waiting to be served seemed to serpentine around a portion of the front tables. Greg went to the rear and then looked at her.

"I know what I want, go check out the displays and see what appeals to you."

From the large display shelves, the bakery served everything. And the aroma of freshly baked pastries had her mouth watering in no time. Even though there was a line, it seemed to move fast.

By the time Greg was at the counter, she'd decided.

They gave their order and stepped to the left to pick it up when ready.

"Just where do you plan to hold this consultation?" she asked, glancing around the crowded establishment. There were no free chairs. Tables were almost stacked on top of one another. Privacy was not a concept the owners obviously grasped.

"Something will open up."

And something did. Just as Greg took their tray, a couple in the back stood.

"Get that table," he ordered.

Abby almost dashed to the back, beating out a young man by inches. She smiled apologetically and then almost giggled when Greg sat down beside her, triumphantly.

"Gotta be fast here," he said, placing her croissant and coffee in front of her.

"I guess. How did you find this place? It doesn't seem like you," she murmured, taking a sip of the coffee. In that, he'd been right—it was the best she'd had in ages!

"I found it one day a long time ago—when I was starting out. You can eat a lot for a little."

"And you had to watch pennies?" she scoffed.

He met her gaze and nodded. "I had a lot of loans. Don't forget, surgeons have to go for extra training. It's only in the last few years that I feel comfortable."

She nodded, suddenly feeling foolish. Just because she'd never known him before he'd become successful didn't mean he hadn't had to work hard to get where he was. She was still paying off student loans she'd taken to cover the difference between expenses and her scholarships. It seemed odd that she and this successful man had that in common.

* * *

Greg watched her eat and almost turned away before she saw what her sensual enjoyment of the food was doing to him. He'd exercised remarkable restraint so far—not even suggesting any interest in her date with Derek. Yet he burned to know if she'd enjoyed herself. Would she bring it up, or was he going to— if he could figure out a way to do it casually?

Had Derek kissed her?

Anger slammed through him at the thought. He didn't want her kissing anyone but him!

Whoa. He took a swallow of coffee and looked away from the delectable sight of her savoring her croissant. He'd never liked a dog-in-the-manger—so why was he acting the role? She was young, pretty and sexy as could be. And up-front about her goal— a relationship that led to marriage.

And he was equally opposed to the institution, so why was he spending time with her?

He'd suggested breakfast to make sure he knew if Derek stayed the night. Not that he expected it. From her inexperienced kisses, he suspected the delectable doctor didn't sleep around. Especially after a first date.

For a moment he considered what he knew about her and a startling thought occurred.

He looked at Abby in confusion.

"What?" she asked, meeting his gaze.

"Are you a virgin?"

Chapter Ten

The people at the next table looked up.

Abby blushed a fiery red and glared at him. "Want to get a microphone so you can repeat the question loud enough for the entire bakery to hear you?" she hissed, leaning forward to keep her voice between them.

He glanced around, met the eyes of the man in the next table and frowned. The man quickly looked away.

"First of all, it's none of your business!" Making sure he heard every word, she continued to glare at him.

Greg liked the way her eyes sparkled, blue and fiery. The pink in her cheeks deepened the color. Would she look like this in the midst of a different kind of passion? Narrowing his eyes in assessment, he wondered what the chances were of ever finding out. Probably slim to none if he continued along these lines. A woman liked finesse.

But one look at Abigail Trent, and finesse was forgotten.

"Second, I can't believe you asked me—especially here where the entire world is practically in our laps! Besides being a totally outrageous, uncalled-for, none-of-your-business question, your lack of sensitivity is totally amazing!"

She took a deep breath. "And third—"

"I'm sorry. You're right—the place was wrong."

"The question was wrong!"

How could a hiss sound as loud as a shout, he wondered.

Nodding once, he leaned closer, almost brushing the hair covering her ear as he spoke softly. "I should have figured it out earlier."

"Look, Dr. Hastings, I agreed to come discuss the conference, not my love life."

He liked seeing her flustered.

"Or lack thereof," he murmured.

Tightening her lips, she looked as if she was about to jump up and storm out of the place.

In the midst of it all, he found it hard to believe. She was thirty years old, and pretty as could be. How had she lived this long without—

"If you want to discuss the conference, okay, if not, I'm going home!"

He'd leave it for the moment. But they'd be back to this fascinating topic. Here was another puzzle to unravel concerning Abby. And he found he was more fond of puzzles than he ever suspected.

"Professor Billingworth had to cancel. We need to find a replacement speaker for his section," he said.

She looked at him. Her color gradually returned to normal, the fiery sparkle fading from her eyes.

"He was speaking on new techniques in brain cancer detection, wasn't he?"

Greg nodded, sipping his coffee, feeling as if he'd just brushed through a conflagration without getting singed. Still time, he knew, but for now, she was staying.

"So are we trying to fill the slot with the same topic, get another expert in that field, or what?"

"Fill the slot, but not necessarily on that topic. We have to move fast, the deadline for sending the programs to the printer is next week. The conference is less than a month away now."

She leaned back and looked at him warily. "What do you expect me to do? I don't know any eminent physicians. I—"

"Throw out suggestions, for one thing. I don't know everyone who is speaking. But I've heard of them or their work. Here's your chance to add something to the lineup that you'd like to see at the conference. Any ideas?"

Slowly she became lost in thought. After a moment she said, "Can I think on it for a day? I want to review the program as it stands and see if there's something that would fit in." She flicked him a glance. "That's why I should have brought the folder. I could have looked at it here and answered today."

"We'll go back to your place when we finish eating and review it there."

Her gaze grew suspicious, but she didn't say anything. Greg almost smiled. He wanted to follow up on his discovery, but would take it slowly. No scaring her off before he found out exactly what he wanted to know.

"Pam's invited Elise and me for lunch. Want to join us?" he asked casually.

"I saw your sisters yesterday. I'm sure they wanted today to be family."

He hadn't known she'd seen Pam and Elise yesterday.

"Why?"

"Why a family lunch? I don't know, they're your sisters."

"No, why did you see both of them yesterday?"

"They came over to help me get ready for my date with Derek. I guess they thought I couldn't manage on my own."

"So how was the date?" he asked as casually as he could muster. He didn't want to hear she'd enjoyed herself, but couldn't stand the suspense any longer.

She raised her eyebrows and made a show of looking at her watch. "My, my, Doctor, you showed remarkable restraint. We've been together almost an hour and a half and this is the first evidence of interest you've shown in my evening with Derek Williams."

He shrugged, holding her gaze. "My primary concern was already answered. I can wait to hear the rest."

"What primary concern?"

"Whether he stayed the night or not."

Realization dawned. "You invited me to an early breakfast to make sure he wasn't there?"

"I invited you to breakfast to discuss the conference."

"I don't believe this! You're far too nosy for your own good, Greg Hastings." She pushed back her chair, but he was quicker. Assuring himself she was finished, he rose and took her hand in his, gripping firmly enough to keep her in place.

"Let go," she said, glancing around to make sure no one was watching. He complied instantly.

"I'll take you home and you can yell at me all you want there. Privacy and all."

"I don't want you in my apartment."

"Even to discuss the conference?"

"You're using that as an excuse."

"So?"

Glancing around once more, she closed her lips tightly and began to walk regally to the front. He tossed a couple of dollars on the table and followed as she wove her way through the crowd.

Reaching the sidewalk, she refused to say a word, but marched to his car. At least she wasn't taking another blasted cab, he thought as he opened the door for her. Did that mean they'd made progress?

Probably only that without her purse she didn't have the means to get home by herself.

The short ride was accomplished in total silence. Reaching her apartment, he half expected her to slam the door in his face, but she merely walked through and left it open behind her. He stepped inside and shut it.

"What do you want to deal with first, the conference or us?" he asked as he joined her in the living room. She had her hands on her hips and had turned to face him.

"There is no us."

He stepped close enough that he could breathe in her fragrance, light and fresh. Her eyes were bright blue, her mouth damp where she'd licked her lips. The sight sent a charge of desire straight where it was most unwelcome. He should have worn looser jeans. Or the pleated dress trousers he wore to work.

"I offered to help you out."

"Introduce me to some friends."

"Well, that was before I realized…" He trailed off. He had been blunt before, but he knew from dealing with his sisters that women didn't like such bluntness.

"Before you found out I've never slept with anyone," she snapped. "What difference does that make to you?"

Suddenly he wondered the same thing. The thought was crushed when he imagined what it would be to initiate Abby into the joys of lovemaking. To be the first man to make sure her pleasure was assured. To not only taste those luscious lips, but every inch of her body. Tangle his fingers in that silky soft hair and press skin to skin.

He'd never made love with a virgin. Even Michelle had had some experience when they'd begun dating. Suddenly he realized the age-old masculine possessiveness of having one woman—to know forever that he'd been the only one with her.

Struck by the irrational thought, he frowned. That belonged to someone who planned to make a lifelong commitment. He was definitely not that someone.

"How—"

She crossed her arms over her chest and looked away. "It's long and involved and not particularly interesting. Just as it's none of your business."

"I'm curious."

"Stay curious."

"Abby." He reached out to draw her closer, feeling

the warmth of her body. She didn't resist, but still refused to look at him.

"You are a beautiful woman. You're smart, and intelligent. I assume this is your choice, I'm just curious. Tell me."

She glanced at him, searching his eyes as if looking for something.

Pushing gently against him until he released her, she turned and walked beside the sofa, as if putting up barriers.

"It's not all entirely by choice. I almost—" She shrugged and took a deep breath.

She did that every time she was nervous. Did she realize she telegraphed her feelings so blatantly?

"It's dumb."

"I doubt it," he said slowly, almost afraid to say anything lest it stop her.

"When I was in high school there was this boy. Terry Bolton. He was everything a girl wanted—popular, terrific looking, had his own car, money to spend and a reputation around the school as one of the biggest catches ever. He dated a bunch of different girls. Then, one day, he turned his attention on me. I was thrilled. We dated. I was in love. He seemed to be. Everything went along perfectly for three weeks." She grimaced.

Greg didn't move, but he had the feeling he wouldn't like what was coming.

"Then things changed. Terry began pressuring me for sex. I mean, we were kissing and everything." She paused and looked at Greg. "Though I have to say they were nothing like the kisses we've shared."

He felt the surprise physically. The desire spread until every inch of him wanted to hold her, kiss her, feel her against him. But he held still, waiting for her to continue.

"Anyway, we went to a party one night. The punch was spiked. It didn't do either of us any good, but we imbibed to our hearts' content. Then we went parking. Terry pushed some more and finally I gave in. I thought I loved him, you see."

He nodded, his fists clenching. The only thing that kept him from hunting up this Terry character and punching him out was the fact he knew she was still a virgin. So what had happened?

She took another deep breath. Even after all this time it was embarrassing. "Only, we couldn't. Actually, Terry couldn't. And he blamed me. Wait," she said when he opened his mouth. "I know now that it was probably the alcohol inhibiting his responses just as it released my inhibitions, but at sixteen, I wasn't so knowledgeable. I believed the things he said about how I couldn't attract anyone, that I was nothing, that a guy couldn't ever get it up for me. And it didn't stop there—by the next afternoon it was all over the school."

Color stained her cheeks again and Greg had an overwhelming urge to jump over the sofa and take her in his arms. But once again he maintained his control.

She shrugged, looked away. "It's an awful thing for a girl to hear when she's finally found enough courage to try it. I guess you could say Terry has been the best birth control ever."

"Traumatic situations as teenagers can affect us all our lives. But surely during college? During med school, when you had to know he'd been a fool and was lashing out at you due to his own frustration."

"Well, by then, I had to study to keep my scholarships, and work hard to make ends meet. I didn't have a lot of time for social activities. And dating never figured high. Plus, Carol and Jeb and I became best friends.''

''So after all this time, you're waiting for Mr. Right.''

She shook her head ruefully. ''Not necessarily. If things had been different, I might think that way. But Carol's death shook me. She was my age, just thirty. Now she's gone. The accident pointed out how quickly life can be over. I want to enjoy it, cherish new experiences, take changes. Really live. I'd hate to be in a car crash next week and have missed everything.''

''Going out with the Dereks of the world will give you the wrong kind of experience,'' Greg said, understanding a bit more the mystery that was Abigail Trent.

''Well, I'm open for suggestions.''

Was this the opening he wanted? ''I'll give you experience.''

She blinked. ''What did you say?''

''I'll give you experience.''

''How much?'' she asked warily.

''As much as you want,'' he said quietly. Instead of introducing her to men who would take advantage of her, he'd show her what to expect.

''Are you looking to get me in bed?'' she asked suspiciously.

The thought flashed through his mind that it would be the worst thing for her. And maybe the best thing in the world for him.

''No.'' The lie sounded false, but she seemed placated.

And it wasn't his intent. It had passed through his mind a while back, but now he wanted her in a different way. Sure he'd love to take her to bed. Love to spend nights in her arms, tutor her in all the ways of love between a man and a woman. But women expected more than just a romp in the sheets. They wanted commitment, caring, some emotional tie. And he couldn't give her that. He couldn't give anyone that.

"Unless you want to," he added. He had to, just in case she wanted more experience than he thought she needed.

The phone rang, shattering the tension that had begun to build. He turned around and headed for the window, giving her a modicum of privacy and trying to get his own thoughts under some control. The idea of tutoring Abigail Trent in the art of dating had a lot of appeal. And would probably end up a lesson in frustration. Already he wanted to kiss her, hold her, mold her body against his and savor the feeling of her breasts pressed against his chest, of the soft cradle of her thighs against him. To taste her, smell her, touch her.

"Hello? Jeb?"

Greg spun around, his gaze going directly to Abby. The infamous Jeb. He still hadn't heard the full story on this man.

"No, but thanks anyway…. I've got plans… I see, well, I'm sorry it didn't work out. No, actually, I'm uh, seeing someone right now." She darted a glance at Greg, then looked away almost guiltily. "He's here now. We've already made plans for today. We'll have to see…bye."

"Jeb Stuart?" Greg asked as she put down the re-

ceiver. He suddenly felt almost primordial. He didn't
want her talking with an old friend who had hurt her.

She nodded.

"What's the story with him?"

"He's a friend."

"The one you dressed up for at the banquet."

She tilted her head, considering him but refusing to
answer his comment. "If your reason for breakfast
wasn't totally bogus, let's look at the conference
stuff."

"Changing the subject?"

She nodded and went to get her folder of conference
material.

Abby couldn't believe she'd told Greg about the
dreaded secret of her past. She'd only ever shared that
with Carol. But his guess at the bakery had startled
her. And since he already knew what she'd hidden
from the rest of the world, she didn't see any big mistake in confiding why.

Though it sounded silly when she discussed it. He
must think she was the dumbest blonde on the planet.

Was that why he felt obligated to make his offer of
providing experience? For a glorious moment she'd
thought he'd sweep her into his arms and carry her
into the bedroom. She'd wondered frantically if she'd
made the bed that morning.

But then he'd clarified the situation. He didn't want
to take her to bed. Words meant little. Action was
what counted. He'd take her on a couple of dates,
probably to make sure she wouldn't make a fool of
him with the men he'd introduce her to. They'd expect
a certain level of sophistication.

Sighing softly, she located the conference folder and

drew it from her purse. He might say Terry had not meant his scathing words, but there had been no lusty, passionate men since then to sweep her away—including Greg. Maybe there had been a bit of truth in Terry's caustic comments.

She spread the conference notes on the coffee table, sitting gingerly on the edge of the chair. Try as she might, she couldn't help noticing Greg when he sat on the sofa. The jeans molded his long legs like a second skin. The shirt faithfully followed every curve of his muscular chest and shoulders. His fingers fascinated her.

"I don't get it. What would you get out of such an arrangement?" she blurted out.

He met her gaze, hesitating a long moment. "I want you," he said slowly, clearly.

Her eyes widened and she stared at him in silence. There was no mistaking the words. Greg Hastings had just told her he wanted her. *Her,* Abigail Trent!

She hadn't a clue what to say. No one had ever been so forthright. Or sent her senses into a tailspin. From the rapid increase of her heart rate to the blood pounding through her veins to the scarcity of air in the room, she felt totally changed by his announcement.

When she remained silent, he grew amused. "I never knew that was a surefire way to shut someone up."

"I don't know what to say."

"You don't have to say anything."

"You can't."

"Can't?"

"Want me. I mean, we hardly know each other and I'm sure not your type."

"And what is my type?"

"I don't know—sophisticated, worldly, cynical."

"If that's true, you are definitely not my type. You are light-years away from cynical. But maybe you're throwing me into a role I don't fit. Maybe you are exactly my type."

She shook her head, a touch of panic flaring. "We don't know each other well enough to...to..."

"To embark on a wild, passionate affair?"

She nodded. She didn't do wild, passionate affairs— everyone knew that.

"I'm not going to push you into something you don't want. You call the shots, Abby. But I wanted no misunderstandings. I'm not that Terry, nor Jeb Stuart."

"Jeb?" She half smiled. "No, you're nothing like Jeb. I'm not going to jump into bed with you."

"As I said, you call the shots. But I wanted you to know where I stand. No misunderstandings, no coy dancing around the facts. You're an intriguing, desirable woman and I want you."

How was anyone supposed to function when all they could do was imagine tangled sheets, entwined limbs and hot, wild sex?

Late that afternoon Abby sat in a wicker rocker on Pam's patio and studied Greg from behind her sunglasses. She'd been doing it all afternoon and didn't feel a step closer to understanding the man.

How had she ended up at Pam's? she wondered. How had she let herself be talked into anything, knowing the man was interested in her in a way no other man had been?

He'd been attentive since they'd left her apartment, but not overly so. In fact, if she were an outsider, she'd wonder if he'd really said what he'd said. His manner was casual and impersonal, his conversation smooth and normal—no sexual innuendos or suggestions.

Yet the shimmering sense of awareness, of being attuned to him as she'd been to no one before, didn't dissipate. She knew where he was with her eyes closed. The ride in the car had been a mix of secret delight and terror. The visit with his sisters peculiar. What wolf on the prowl brought his prey to join his family for lunch?

Yet that was almost how she felt. He'd set his sights on her. Where would it all end?

She knew nothing about being alluring to the opposite sex. She'd perfected a manner of casual friendship with all the men she'd dealt with since Terry, hiding the hurt his words had caused, and hiding the insecurity they'd fostered.

Now this blatantly sexy, dynamic man had told her he wanted her!

How was she supposed to deal with that? Especially when he then acted as if she was no more to him than one of his sisters.

Or was it camouflage? Was he lulling her into a sense of complacency so better to pounce?

For a moment she thought it would be rather nice to be pounced on.

The notion shocked her. She glanced around, but no one seemed to have any indication of her thoughts. Especially Greg. Thank goodness.

It was hard to concentrate on anything with his statement echoing in her mind.

When Elise asked about Derek and the infamous date, she smiled and said it was nice.

Pam laughed. "That's the first time I've heard Derek called nice. A lot of other names, but not nice."

"Isn't he nice?" Abby asked.

"Oh sure, like a snake," Greg murmured.

"Not that bad, brother dearest. Derek knows how to show a woman a good time," Elise defended.

"And I had a nice time," Abby said, darting a glance at Greg. His smoldering gaze sent shivers of excitement dancing along her nerve endings. "Nice, but not memorable. I don't think we'll be going out again."

"I bet Harry asks you out soon. He's a lot of fun," Pam said.

"I hear he can only talk about his last breakup," Elise said, and she looked at Abby.

"His third wife left him," Pam explained.

"At least he got a divorce. You should divorce Dave," Elise said.

Pam shook her head. "If he wants to end the marriage, he has to tell me. Otherwise, he knows where to find me."

"I don't get it. He obviously wants more than you offered, why make it easy on him to come back?"

Abby smiled sympathetically at Pam. "I understand. You and he had something special. Now it's changed, but maybe not for good. If you can, you want what you had. Love's like that, isn't it?"

"Love is an illusion," Greg said sharply.

Abby shook her head, "No, just a difficult emotion to get a handle on. And marriage isn't something that ends with the wedding ceremony. It takes work all along—both parties trying to make it."

Pam nodded. "Exactly. If I felt overwhelmed with things and went off to find myself and decided what

I had was pretty darn good, I'd want Dave to be there when I returned.''

Elise frowned. ''I think you're both romantic fools. Letting a man take advantage of you doesn't show any kind of love, just that you're a doormat.''

''Hey, it's not limited to women,'' Greg said.

''True, women like Michelle should wear a sign— dangerous predator.''

Abby listened to the interchange with sadness. She wanted the kind of love Pam recognized, not the faithless emotion Greg and Elise discussed. And if a person couldn't find it, was it better to go along without, or find something in the meantime to substitute?

Like an affair with a sexy, cynical doctor? she asked herself.

Twice Abby caught Greg's gaze on her. Did his sisters suspect he wanted more from Abby than it appeared on the surface? If so, neither gave a hint, though she did catch Elise's speculative look at one point during the afternoon.

Bethany, Pam and Dave's daughter, returned home in time for dinner. The affection between Greg and his niece was unexpected. Bethany teased him and had him laughing in a genuine fashion—no cynicism when he dealt with her. Wistfully Abby wished for the same when he dealt with her!

And she felt she got her way when he took her home. No passionate kisses, no lingering goodbyes. She felt like a niece or other family relation. Perplexed, she went to bed wondering why, on the one hand, he purported to want her, and yet could bid her good-night so casually.

Maybe she'd make more sense of it in the morning.

Chapter Eleven

The next few days passed in a whirl. Abby and Greg met for lunch on Monday ostensibly to plan for the conference replacement, but he'd already come up with a tentative replacement speaker and Abby was content to go along with his recommendation. She'd spent far more time Sunday thinking about Greg than any substitute physician.

Tuesday in the staff meeting, she sat as far from him as she could without causing comment. She couldn't trust herself in such close proximity, not when her dreams had been strangely erotic during the past two nights.

Susan caught her after the meeting to follow up on a patient and Abby thankfully latched on to her friend, half-afraid Greg would say something outrageous in front of the entire staff. He looked at her as they hurried by, yet remained silent.

But he was waiting for her in her office when she returned. Closing the door, he deliberately stepped close enough that she could feel his body heat, feel her space invaded.

"Avoiding me, Abigail?" he asked. His fingers came up to toy with a loose strand of hair and she had to grit her teeth to keep from doing something silly.

"Not at all, Doctor, why would you think that?"

"From the way you have of disappearing the past couple of days anytime I come into view."

"I am busy."

"Too busy to have dinner tonight?"

"Tonight?" Instantly visions of their last kiss filled her mind. Her gaze dropped to his lips and she could almost feel the scorching heat. She felt herself inching closer, then stopped. They were in her office at the hospital, for heaven's sake.

"Dinner," he prompted, the gleam in his eyes suggesting he had an idea of her thoughts.

"When and where?"

"We can go as soon as you finish with your last patient. I'll follow you home and we'll take my car from there. Like Chinese?"

"Sure." Her heart began pounding. She was agreeing to a real date with Greg Hastings. Dangerous to her peace of mind. For once she didn't care. *Excitement, here I come!*

The afternoon seemed to drag. Abby was thankful her last patient had a minor ailment and was soon diagnosed, treated and dismissed. She was ready to leave.

Hesitating just a moment, she dialed Greg's extension. He answered on the first ring.

"I'm leaving now."

"Head for home, I'll swing by and pick you up in a few minutes."

It would give her time to freshen up after a day at work. "Deal. See you there."

Brushing her hair a short time later, Abby gazed at herself in her bathroom mirror. She had not felt this excited when going out with Derek. In fact she had almost dreaded that evening. But this—a casual, spur-of-the-moment date had her nervous and seething with anticipation.

When Greg knocked a few minutes later, she was ready.

"You look nice," he said, letting his gaze drift over her.

"What's wrong?" She knew instantly he was tired and distracted.

"Nothing. I'm ready to eat if you are."

"As soon as you tell me why you seem so tired." Almost dispirited.

He shrugged, waiting as she closed the door. They stepped into the elevator before he spoke again. "Gall bladder op didn't go so well today. The patient isn't responding. Has post-op complications. I'm trying a different med. I told the nurses to call if there was any change either way."

"Would you rather skip tonight?"

He looked at her and slowly shook his head. "I'm expecting you to cheer me up with your rose-colored-glasses view of the world."

"I'll do my best. Which is all we can ever do, right?"

"Spare me the platitudes. I want the patient to recover. Not hear how we do the best we can."

"We do," she said softly.

"Just be warned I may not make it through to dessert."

"I won't throw a tantrum if you don't. I understand, remember?"

"Which is more than Michelle ever did."

"Or Derek. Did I tell you I got a call on Saturday night and he was thoroughly annoyed by it."

Greg opened the door for his car, laughing softly. "A first for Derek. He usually considers himself quite the ladies' man."

"Then I question the sensibilities of the women in this city," she said with some asperity.

In only a few minutes they followed the waiter to a quiet alcove at a Chinese restaurant on Grant Avenue. Abby's mouth watered at the delectable aromas that filled the place. The menu had dozens of choices. She glanced at Greg over the top of the page. He looked tired, discouraged. She had the strangest longing to soothe away the frown that marred his face, to massage his temples and see if he could relax. She knew he'd done his best. It was now up to a higher power to determine whether or not his patient would recover.

But she also knew that never stopped doctors from doing all they could—including worrying about each patient.

Maybe he wasn't as cynical as she thought. He cared about his patient. Why was his reputation so different at the hospital? Did he deliberately foster an image contrary to his true feelings?

The expected call came as they were finishing dinner.

"Timing was good tonight," she said genially as he rose to find a pay phone when the beeper summoned.

By the time he returned, she had already asked for the check.

"A woman who does understand," he said, settling the bill and waiting for her to slip out of the booth.

"Do you have to go in?"

"Yes. If I can't figure out what's not working, I might have to open him back up. Something is not right."

"Then let me get a cab and you go straight to the hospital, no sense in taking time to go out of your way."

"I'll drop you."

"No, Greg, I'll manage."

She could see he was torn, but finally nodded. "Thanks, Abby, you're—"

He leaned over and kissed her hard on her mouth, then released her to tell the valet attendant to find the lady a cab. He got into his car when it drew up and headed for the hospital, his mind already on the patient, Abby knew.

She watched him drive away. The kiss had not been what she'd expected or hoped for. Brief, almost impersonal, it was nothing like the last one they'd shared, with tongues, teeth and heat. But still, it sent a tingle through her. The sappy grin she gave to the parking attendant when he opened the cab door told her she was in danger of losing more than her equilibrium with the dashing doctor.

Restless as the evening progressed, Abby searched for the paper Greg had written his phone number on in her office. She knew she'd stuffed it into her purse.

Locating it triumphantly a minute later, she took a deep breath and dialed his number. She expected the answering machine.

"Hi Greg, it's Abby. Call me when you get home, no matter how late! I want to hear about your patient."

She hung up. Would he call? Or would he use the late hour as an excuse?

It was late when the phone rang, or rather, early in the morning, she thought as she glanced at the glowing dial of her clock.

"Hello?"

"You said call. It's late. I know I woke you."

"Yes, but that's okay, I wanted you to. How's your patient?"

"Still touch-and-go. I elected not to reopen."

"How old is he?"

"He's sixty-seven. Been in poor health for a while. But I thought he was strong enough for the operation. So did his referring physician."

"You've done all you can," she said gently.

"Yeah, I guess."

Silence hummed on the line.

"It's times like these that I hate living alone," he said suddenly.

"I know. Even a cat or dog would help, wouldn't it?"

"Or a beautiful woman."

"You must be feeling better."

"A little. Are you in that sexy teddy?"

"You're feeling a lot better. Get some sleep, Doctor."

"That's your prescription, sleep?"

"That's it. Oatmeal and orange juice in the morning."

"How about I take two aspirins and call you back?"

"Good night, Greg!"

"Good night, Abby," he said at last. "And thanks."

Snuggling beneath her covers, she hoped talking to him had been a help. But it was tough to be alone when things didn't go right. She'd had Carol and Jeb for so long. Who would she turn to now, if she had a bad day?

Sharing the problem made Greg all the more human—and all the more appealing.

Abby called Greg's office the next morning, but Rose only said he wasn't there. Her own patient load was such she was busy throughout the day. A number of new chicken pox cases had her worried about a mini-epidemic, and she had a talk with the public health office to report her findings and get updated information from other physicians in the city.

It was five-thirty before she knew it. Trying Greg's office once more, she wasn't surprised to hear Rose answer again. The woman seemed to live at the hospital.

"I just wanted to see how his patient was," Abby said, determined to get an answer before going home.

"Which one?" Rose asked.

"The gall bladder operation from yesterday."

"Mr. Jenkins died this afternoon," Rose said slowly. "Greg left for home not long after talking with the family."

"I see." Her heart ached. No doctor liked losing a patient—ever!

She started to dial his number, then hesitated. If he'd wanted her to know, he would have called, she reasoned. She picked up the small stack of phone messages—nothing from Greg.

She cleared her desk and headed for her car, all the

time arguing with herself. She had no reason to suspect he'd like to hear from her, to see her. Granted
he'd thrown out that outrageous comment about wanting her last Sunday, but he'd done nothing to follow
up on it. Had it been his way to mitigate some of
Terry's damage? A kindness for a fellow physician?

She reached her apartment and hurried up to
change. Gathering the ingredients she needed to make
a quick dish, she headed back out. She'd see if he
wanted dinner and company. If not, she'd know she
tried.

Greg lived in one of the high-rise apartment buildings near the Marina. Depending which floor he was
on, he would have a terrific view, she thought as she
sought parking. San Francisco was never an easy city
in which to find parking, and especially now, when
she was so anxious.

When she rang his doorbell five minutes later, she
wondered what he'd do when he saw her—slam the
door in her face or invite her in.

He opened the door and stared at her.

"What are you doing here?"

He didn't sound angry. And the door was still open.

"I came to fix you dinner. Unless you've already
eaten?"

"No." After a moment, he stepped aside.

He still wore his suit trousers and white shirt, the
tie loosened and hanging crookedly. He'd rolled back
his sleeves so his forearms were bare.

Stopping just inside, Abby glanced around, looking
for the kitchen. The apartment went beyond trendy.
Everything looked like chrome and glass with black
leather as an accent.

"I thought you'd be into leather," she murmured, finding the decor stark and unappealing.

He looked around and shrugged. "Michelle decorated the place. When she left, I didn't change much. I'm not home that much to care."

"Where's the kitchen?" Abby would not get into a discussion of his ex-wife and her taste. Or lack thereof.

"Over there. Why are you here, Abby?"

She ignored her own question along that line and headed as indicated. "I heard from Rose that Mr. Jenkins died. I'm sorry, Greg."

"Me, too."

He followed her into the kitchen, leaning against the counter and looking at her. "But I've had other patients die over the years. Why are you here?"

"I didn't know you then. Now I do. I thought you might like some company."

She unloaded the bag and opened three drawers before finding a knife. She began to cut up the meat.

"Can you find me a large frying pan? You do have pans, don't you?" She looked up.

"Yes. What are you making?"

"Paella. It's good and fast and different. I know you like rice, you ate it at the Chinese place."

"I love rice." He located a pan and put it on the stove for her. Leaning back against the spotless counter, he folded his arms across his chest, watching her efficient movements.

"I still don't understand why you're here."

"I thought you could use a friend," she said, concentrating on preparing the food, almost afraid to meet his eyes.

He was silent for a moment. "Are we friends?"

"Sort of," she said, risking a glance at him. "I

mean if a man says he wants someone, isn't that a kind of friendship?''

He shook his head, his eyes never leaving her. ''Seduction has nothing to do with friendship.''

''Oh. Well, that's all right then. I have nothing to do with seduction. But I do make a great friend, ask Jeb.''

''Jeb?''

''When he called Sunday it was to see if I wanted to hang out again. Apparently the blond bombshell dumped him.''

''So he ran straight for you again. Maybe he came to his senses.''

''What he realized is that we are friends and when people feel bad, they want friends around to cheer them up.''

''Your naiveté scares me.''

''I'm not naive, at least not in that. I think you're the one who doesn't let people get close. Everyone needs friends, Greg.''

''I thought you considered Jeb the love of your life. Wasn't that what all the new clothes are about?''

''We're friends. I know that now. And should have known it all along.''

''Thinking back, I don't remember your offering me a lot of friendship.''

''How can you say that? We act like friends—I took your advice and got help from Pam and Elise. I told you things in my past no one else knows. That's friendship.''

He studied her curiously. ''No one else knows about Terry?''

She shook her head. ''Carol did, but she's dead.''

''You never told Jeb?''

She shook her head, wondering why they were talking about this. If he wanted her, couldn't he at least have given her a kiss, brushed his fingertips across her shoulders, tugged on her hair, said something suggestive?

She was growing nervous with his never-moving gaze. Fortunately she'd finished cutting. She should have had him do that part, he was the surgeon. She almost giggled at her rationale. He'd probably be horrified.

"What?" he asked, noticing her amusement.

"I just thought you should have cut the meat, you have more experience."

"So then what would you do, diaper it?"

She laughed and faced him head-on. "No, I'd cook it. Just like I'm going to do now. If you want salad or something to go with it, you're in charge. I didn't have any fixings at home so didn't bring anything beyond what I needed for the paella."

"I'm not very hungry." The haunted look returned.

"You'll discover how hungry you are when you taste this delicious meal," she went on blithely. He'd forgotten for a couple of minutes, she knew he had. She wanted to make him forget a little longer.

"There are different kinds of hunger," he said, reaching out to pull her into his arms.

His kiss exploded on her senses like fireworks on the Fourth of July. At last! She dropped the spoon and wrapped her arms around him, holding on tightly. She knew he was anguished by the loss of a patient. If she could give him some respite, good.

Only *respite* was the wrong word. There was nothing restful or relaxing about his kiss. Her blood thundered in her head. Her skin felt six sizes too small, but the tingling sensations that danced through her had her forgetting that. Forgetting everything. She could only focus on the sheer delight his mouth evoked.

He kissed her like a starving man too long alone in the desert. She was drunk on excitement, intoxicated in pleasure. His body called to hers and she responded.

When he moved to trace his lips along the edge of her jaw a flash of sanity returned.

"We either stop, or I turn off the stove," she said, amazed she could hold a cognizant thought. She wanted to delve into him and never come up for air.

Without a word, he flipped off the burner and reached beneath her knees to lift her. In less than a minute, they stopped by a huge bed in his dimly lit bedroom. Abby knew he couldn't see her. Maybe her silhouette, but nothing more. Nothing more than she could see, which was not enough.

Still, she could feel. When his lips found hers again, she gave herself up to those feelings. This was life, pulsating through every cell. For a time they could hide from death, reaffirm the precious freedom to taste and touch and feel. To live.

She felt vulnerable, naive just as he'd called her. Was he as caught up in these explosive sensations as she?

His hands raised to her shoulders, softly closing on her. "Did you wear that sinful silk teddy tonight?" he whispered as his fingers moved gently over the cotton of her casual top, slipping fingers beneath the neckline to caress the skin beneath.

She shook her head, her heart pounding. She should tell him the truth—there was no teddy—but the words wouldn't come. What would he say if she told him? Would he scoff at her for trying to sound sexy? Or suggest they remedy the situation immediately and go buy it?

His hands moved and gathered up her hair, brushing strands through his fingers, rubbing it with his thumb. "I've wanted to do this since you got it lightened. You smell like sunshine and wildflowers," he said so softly Abby almost didn't hear him. Then he lowered his mouth against hers again and kissed her long and deeply.

She was breathing hard when he pulled back enough to rest his forehead against hers. She could almost make out his eyes in the darkness.

"Be sure, Abigail. I don't want to do anything you don't want. I can still stop."

She couldn't breathe. She couldn't hear for the fiery blood roaring in her ears. Didn't he have any idea what he did to her? He was a doctor, for heaven's sake. He knew as much about human anatomy as she did. How could he not know he was driving her insane? He wanted her. He'd been clear on that. Wasn't she being equally clear she wanted him? Craved his touch, yearned for completion?

She wanted to strip his shirt off and kiss him all over that hot, muscular chest. She wanted to feel his hands on her, caressing and fondling and driving her insane with the sensations that she knew hovered just beyond the horizon.

See him over her, see how dark his eyes got in the midst of passion. Feel his skin against hers, his breath mingled with hers, his mouth devouring hers like she wanted to do to him.

Maybe it was time to find out if he'd been leading her on. She'd cut to the chase. She just wasn't sure how yet, but they'd made a start.

He shifted uncomfortably, and Abby felt a hard ridge press against her. She, who had never been considered a desirable woman, savored the knowledge. His hand rubbed her back, tracing her spine, pulling her tighter.

Slowly she relaxed, permitting herself to enjoy. His hand on her lower back kept her pressed against his length. Abby felt his hard legs brush hers, igniting fiery tendrils of awareness. The fingers of his left hand threaded through her hair again, holding her for another kiss. Abby felt the steady beat of his heart beneath her fingers. His hand at her back moved up and pressed her breasts against his chest. Abby felt as if they soared on clouds.

"You drive me crazy," he murmured against her mouth. "Are you sure?"

"Never so sure in my life!"

Abby reveled in the heat from his body enveloping her, caressing her, inflaming her. His long legs were spread to hold him, them. His chest was solid against the softness of her breasts.

When his lips swooped to claim her they weren't soft and gentle, but hot and demanding. She hadn't known a kiss could be so shattering. Her whole body was caught up with the pleasure his mouth and tongue wrought. Giving a soft murmur in the back of her throat, she longed for even more, pressing herself greedily against him as her mouth moved ardently against his. She'd never known such enchantment. Her legs were like jelly, her body hot and fevered, yearning for Greg Hastings. Every cell exploded with sensory overload.

Her tongue met his, mated, danced, coupled with his. She had never before felt such ecstasy. She was enthralled. Greedy, she wanted more. Did she offer him the same mindless delight he brought her?

The kiss slowed, deepened. He pulled back slightly, still cradling her face in his hands. His eyes glittered with suppressed emotion and he stared down at her for long silent seconds, taking in her soft lips swollen and damp from his kiss, her erratic breathing. His thumbs gently brushed against her rosy, inflamed cheeks.

Without a word, he picked her up and placed her gently on the bed.

"I just hope it works," she said, suddenly remembering Terry.

"Trust me, it'll work. Do you want a light to undress?" he murmured, reaching for her in the darkness.

"You're the surgeon, I thought you had talented hands," she murmured as she arched up to assist him in removing her top.

He eased the cotton shirt up her slender body, slipping it over her head before his hands brushed against her skin, tracking a line of fiery ice to the tip of each breast. Caressing each mound gently, he teased her nipples until they were ready. Then he put his hot mouth over one and tasted her.

"I can't believe this," she murmured as she gave in to the intense pleasure pooling between her legs. Her hands sought his buttons, opening his shirt with almost frantic haste. She wanted him so much she was tempted to rip the clothes from his body and demand he love her.

In only seconds they were both bare and pressed against each other.

His hands stroked her, from her silky hair down her smooth warm back to the firm mounds of her bottom.

Slipping his fingers between her legs, he brushed against her, again and again, drawing the heat, building the fire between them until all awkwardness was forgotten.

She moved against him, her breasts pressing into his chest, her legs flanking his hips, the hot center of her beckoning him like a beacon for home. Her kisses were hot and erotic and driving him near the brink. Fumbling in his nightstand, he couldn't find what he was seeking.

"Greg, please." Her lips skimmed across his jaw, fastened on the pulse point beating in his throat. She shifted her hips. He groaned with desire.

"I can't find—there, I've got it." In only seconds he was ready, poised over her, slowly lowering until he breached the slight barrier and Abby drew him deep within.

The sting was slight, the feeling of Greg against her astonishing. How could she have let herself miss something so wonderful for all these years?

He captured one breast in his mouth, his hands stroking her, caressing her, petting her. She felt so hot, so restless, wound tight as a spring about to burst.

"Now, Abby, now!" Her rhythm increased and he moved with her, faster and faster until he went rigid. She cried out as the pleasure pulsed through her, through him. She thought she screamed. She remembered hearing his voice, harsh with emotion, shouting at the last. The endless pulse filled her, had her flying higher than she'd thought possible, and then the heat invaded and swept away every thought but Greg. Clinging desperately, she stretched out the enchantment as long as possible.

Then, slowly, feeling as if she were still floating, Abby sank back on the mattress, breathing hard and fast.

Chapter Twelve

When Abby awoke, she was nestled against Greg, her back resting against his chest, her legs against his. One of his arms was beneath her head, the second reached across her and he cupped her breast. She lay still, enjoying the heat of his body, wondering what he thought about their coming together.

I love you, she thought, then shied away from the idea. She'd been swept up in the lovemaking. That didn't make it love.

Yet she wondered. She'd never done anything like it. Didn't that mean she had some feelings for him? Beyond that for a colleague at work?

"Does this put Terry's words behind you?" he asked softly.

She started, surprised to hear him. "I do believe it does," she said, surprised.

"You're cold," he said as his hands brushed her cooled flesh.

"Only on the outside. Where I'm pressed against you, I'm burning up," she said, stretching lazily, rubbing against him as sensuously as a cat. Slowly she turned, trying to see him in the darkness.

He gave her a quick kiss and pulled the sheet over them.

"Are you hungry?" she asked sleepily.

"I told you there are different kinds of hunger. You've filled one, Abby. I can wait for food."

"How late is it?"

It was completely dark outside. She could see the faint glow of the city lights reflected through the gap in the curtains at the window.

"Not even ten."

"I guess not too late, then, to eat."

Suddenly embarrassed, she wondered what the protocol was for getting out of bed without a stitch on. Especially when the man she was entangled with made no move to get up. Abby wasn't going to make the first move, she decided. Keeping still, she gradually relaxed. If she didn't move soon, she'd fall asleep again.

"Want to take a shower?" he asked softly.

"That'd be nice." How mundane. Shouldn't they be talking of more important things. Like where they went from here?

He released her and rolled to the far side of the bed. She heard him padding across the room. He flipped the light on in the adjacent bath, then crossed to the dresser and pulled out some clothes. Reaching into the closet, he snagged a terry robe and tossed it to the bed.

"You can put that on if you like, or your clothes. I'll use the guest bath."

In two seconds he was gone.

Slowly Abby sat up, feeling the sweet ache of muscles she hadn't known she possessed. Taking the robe, she went into the bathroom. So much for the fleeting thought they'd bathe together. Now that would be erotic! But was that something only lovers did? What precisely was their relationship?

A half hour later she took a deep breath and flung open the bedroom door. She'd donned her clothes, brushed her hair until it shone. There wasn't much she could do about her slightly swollen lips, but she couldn't worry about that.

She'd prepare dinner, eat and run. She knew Greg probably did this kind of thing all the time. And even though he knew it was her first, she would prove she could be up on the rules of the game. No clinging. No discussion of any future! He'd made his position clear.

As she'd made hers.

He was in the kitchen when she entered, in jeans, bare feet and a checked shirt, still unbuttoned.

One glimpse of that chest, the tight abs and trail of dark hair arrowing beneath his waistband and she could do nothing but stop and stare—and feel way overdressed.

He looked at her. Smiling brightly, she headed for the stove and the pan with its olive oil still awaiting heat. The familiar task gave her something to do and she gratefully plunged in.

"No regrets?" he asked, stepping closer, fingering a strand of her hair.

"No." Taking another breath, she dared to look at him. "You?"

"Only that you should have had wine and music and candlelight for your first time."

"Is that what you had?"

He looked startled, then grinned, shaking his head. "No, my first time was in the back of Mary Jane Kolowski's father's Chevy."

"I suspect music and candles are overrated." She wished she could have known Greg when he was a randy teenager. Though he probably wouldn't have looked twice at her.

"I would have, you know."

"What?"

"I would have asked you out."

"How did you know I was thinking that?" She was flabbergasted. Did he read minds?

"Your face is so expressive. Don't ever play poker."

"I'll remember that. You're too close. I need room to cook." She needed room to breathe and that was the basic requirement if she wanted to keep her mind focused.

He set the table while she prepared the paella. When they sat down, the nervousness she still felt didn't dissipate. It might never, she realized with a start. What if she spent the rest of her life nervous around this man? They'd been as intimate as people could be and she was still nervous?

Yes!

She ate quickly. If she finished, she could leave. She needed time and distance to get her emotions under some sort of control. Just making love didn't mean she was in love.

Though maybe a bit infatuated.

"You reached your goal," Greg said when she put her fork down for the last time.

"What?" She looked up, caught by his warm gaze.

"Dr. Taylor won't have to set you up for the charity ball."

"He won't?"

"Nope. You're going with me."

"I am not!"

Greg reached for her hand, lacing his fingers through hers. "Why not? Didn't what just happened mean anything to you?"

"Did it mean anything to you?"

"Yes. Do you think I just hop into bed with anyone who's available?"

Abby didn't respond immediately. Hadn't she thought exactly that. From the dawning annoyance on his face, maybe she'd made an incorrect assumption.

"Not exactly," she said. "But neither do I think we've just bonded for life because of…of…" Floundering, she wasn't even sure what to call what had happened.

Besides spectacular. And astonishing. And fantastic.

"We didn't bond for life. But we could see where this leads."

"Until I find Mr. Right?" she tried for clarity, but it was hard to think with Greg holding her hand, with his thumb tracing patterns on her skin that had her remembering every touch, every caress he'd given in that dark bedroom.

"Until you get all the experience you think you need to begin searching for Mr. Right."

"I don't want to waste any time. I'm not getting younger and if I get hit by a drunk—"

"You're not going to get hit by a drunk driver. You seem to have a fixation about that."

The fixation was more about him! And the craving she had suddenly developed for his touch, for his kisses.

"Not a fixation, but a realization life can end in an instant."

"So have an affair before it does."

An affair?

She tugged her hand free and stood. Gathering her dish, she headed for the kitchen. "I'll think about it and let you know." Just because she wanted to jump into his lap and declare herself his for the duration was no reason to let him know she'd be more than interested in an affair. What had happened to her plan to meet new men, find a mate, start a family?

Put on temporary hold, she admitted, while she explored the wild thing with Dr. Sexy.

If Terry Bolton could only see her now!

He'd wanted to take her home, but she'd insisted she had her car and needed to have it at her place in case she was called in the night. He offered to follow her there, but she'd refused.

The question was, why? He opened the drapes and gazed unseeing out at the sparkling lights of the city. His mind replayed the scene in his bedroom earlier.

She'd been so soft and sweet in his arms, her untutored kisses wildly passionate. She was so unaware of her desirability he couldn't believe it. And he wanted to be the one to tap in to that passion, bring her to her full potential. But then could he walk away?

He would have to. Marriage was not for him. Though it was something she wanted. Why did women think that was such a great institution? Even Michelle had ended up marrying again. Pam held open the belief David would return.

At least Elise had her head on right.

He looked at the phone. Should he call her to see if she had reached home safely? He knew she was a careful driver, though her friend had been, as well, her death resulting from a drunk driver.

Or would a call send the wrong message? Abby seemed to have her head on straight. She didn't make any push for more than he was willing to give. In fact, she seemed just as pleased to go to dinner with Mike Adams as she did with him.

He had a difficult surgery scheduled the next day, time to get some sleep. But slipping between the sheets a few minutes later, he smelled Abby's scent. She invaded his senses and filled his arms with longing. It'd been a long time since he'd missed anyone in bed. He wished she had stayed the night.

Next time, he'd press harder.

The next two days were hectic for Greg. He had a difficult surgery that lasted far longer than originally anticipated. But the outcome seemed assured. He met with two other prospective patients then made the rounds to check on his admitted patients. Nothing took him to Abby's floor, nor near her offices.

Friday he called her first thing upon arriving at the hospital.

"Hi," she said. "I was going to call you. I have a patient, Jimmy Ryan, I want to refer to you, can you take a look at his records and see him?"

They hadn't spoken since Wednesday night and she

wanted to discuss a patient? After thirty years she was no longer a virgin, and she wanted to discuss a patient?

"I called to see how you're doing," he said.

"Fine. Thanks. Anyway, I'm sending Jimmy's folder over. Let me know what you think, okay?"

"I could tell you over lunch."

The silence surprised him. "Lunch?" she almost squeaked.

"The meal at midday."

"I'm busy today. Maybe another time? I've got to run. Let me know about Jimmy, okay?"

Hanging up with some irritation, he rose and went to stare out his window. He had half a mind to go to her office and see what she thought she was doing. But if she was busy, as she said, that would only fuel the gossip mill. And Greg wasn't ready to go there again. They'd done a fine job when he and Michelle had had their trouble.

But he wanted some answers, and he planned to get them today. He could wait until he'd reviewed the folder and then call her back. She could put him off once, but if she thought she could keep doing it, she had a surprise coming.

Abby sank into her desk chair and leaned back. She'd give anything if she could close her eyes and go to sleep. Today had been beyond hectic. If that chicken pox epidemic didn't abate soon, she'd go bonkers. The public health office had issued warnings to the schools, but the number of small children who had not yet had the disease seemed to be high—and all making up for lost time.

The last patient had left only moments ago. Her

nurse was delighted to leave, and Abby wished she could beam herself home and not have to face traffic.

"Abigail?" Greg Hastings stood in the doorway.

She opened her eyes. Another problem.

"Hi." She sat up, debated standing but decided she didn't need to. Besides, her knees were probably too weak to hold her. What was she going to say to the man?

Gesturing to a chair, she said, "Have a seat." She spotted the folder in his hand as he crossed her small office. "Jimmy's file. What do you think?"

He tossed it onto her desk. "I've already called his parents and they'll all be in Monday afternoon. I think your diagnosis is correct, but I want to evaluate him for myself before committing to surgery."

"Fine." She expected nothing less. Relieved he'd take the case, she fidgeted with the notes on her desk. He'd said he'd see Jimmy. She wished he'd leave.

"Dinner?"

She looked up, caught by his dark gaze. Suddenly all the scrambled thoughts she'd tried to suppress over the past couple of days pressed to the forefront of her mind. And all the insecurities and uncertainties.

"Not tonight, thanks." Her gaze dropped to her desk.

"Why not?"

She shrugged. "I'm already busy."

He studied her for a long moment. "Cut to the chase, Abby. What's going on? We shared something special on Wednesday night, and it's now Friday and I've not heard from you."

She fiddled with her pen, darting a quick glance at him.

"Maybe I'm not sure what you're expecting," she said slowly.

"What do you think I'd expect. Didn't we embark on an affair?"

"Did we? And what does that entail? I've never had one before. Are we good friends who sleep together, so spend a lot of time together? Are we exclusive, or do we just date occasionally when one or the other of us has the urge—"

"No, it has nothing to do with getting an urge. I thought we'd spent time together."

"Dating?"

He frowned. "Not only dating. You came to my place the other night when I'd had a rough day. I could come to your place tonight. We could get take-out and not have to cook."

"I already have a date," she said, almost holding her breath.

"With?"

"Mike Adams."

"Cancel."

She hesitated. "I'm not sure I should do that."

He stood. "Then don't. Maybe I misread the situation."

"Wait. What is it you want, Greg?"

"I'm not looking to hop into bed with you every time I see you, if that's what you think," he said.

"You're not?" She was surprised at that. She'd thought that was exactly what he wanted.

He ran his fingers through his hair in frustration. "Abby, you are not just a bed partner. Though I have to say I've had the most erotic dreams the past two nights, featuring you in the starring role."

"So it's my scintillating mind you really find fascinating,'' she drawled, trying to stall. She felt baffled by his comment. Did he really want to spend time with her? Get to know her?

He raised an eyebrow. ''Let's just say I like the whole package—from your scintillating mind to your sexy little body. And I want to know more about both. But if you don't want exclusivity—''

''I do,'' she said quickly.

Before she could think, she punched in Mike's extension. In less than three minutes, she'd canceled the date without a drop of remorse. Mike didn't seem to care.

''Next excuse,'' Greg said cynically. ''You have a headache? You're too tired?''

''I am tired, but not too tired to have you over for dinner.''

''If you're truly tired, I'll leave after we eat. Or if you fall asleep during dinner, it won't be the first time you've found my company so boring you drift off.''

She grimaced, hating to be reminded. It made her feel foolish. ''Okay, if you want to chance it.'' Her heart was pounding. She didn't feel like herself. She never canceled out on friends, or changed her plans on a whim.

But with Greg it felt different. She knew it wouldn't last, so she had to make up her mind quickly.

When they reached her apartment, she went into the bedroom to change into slacks and a loose top. Brushing her hair eased some of the tension in her neck, but she couldn't help feeling a bit anxious with Greg's presence. What if he expected more than she could deliver?

On the other hand, she wasn't sure what he expected. So far he had made no move to kiss her. They could be two casual friends who had decided to share pizza for dinner.

She called in the order, then poured them each a glass of wine. Greg had removed his jacket and tie, and loosened the collar buttons of his shirt before settling in the love seat. He looked across at her as she sat on the wing chair.

"If you got some decent-sized furniture, we could sit together."

"Your sofa's nice," she said, leaning back in her chair and putting her bare feet on the Queen Anne coffee table. "But that love seat suits you."

"I'm lonely in it."

She smiled slowly, liking the suggestive note in his voice. "Maybe after dinner we can play musical chairs or something."

"Or play something. I'm hoping you'll regain some energy with dinner."

"Oh, Doctor, so there is something more you want."

"Besides your mind?"

She nodded.

"So I admit it." He shrugged, his gaze never leaving hers.

"Tell me about your day, but don't tell me why you aren't tired? Unless you can bottle the prevention."

"I had a hell of a day yesterday. In comparison, today was a breeze."

They discussed work, the conversation then moving naturally to other topics. When the pizza arrived, Abby was already feeling more alert and she had yet to eat a bite.

They discussed food likes and dislikes—after agreeing on the combination pizza. Pleased to discover they shared an adventurous streak with trying new foods, she daringly suggested they seek out a few new ethnic restaurants to try over the next few weeks. Amazed when Greg agreed, she began to look forward to the Vietnamese restaurant they settled on for the next night.

When finished, Abby wondered if he'd leave right away. The night was young, tomorrow started the weekend, and food had revived her. But she wasn't sure she wanted him to stay. Not if it meant going to bed. She loved the other night, but was still too uncertain of her own feelings, and her perspective, to give in to her desire. She wanted a better understanding of what she was doing. Where they were going.

"I'm heading for home," he said while she rinsed the plates.

"I'm feeling more awake," she said. Contrarily wishing he'd stay now that he'd made the first move to leave. What was wrong with her?

"You're still tired. Get some sleep. I'll see you tomorrow." He flung an arm around her shoulders and urged her from the kitchen. Snagging his jacket and tie, he walked to the door.

His kiss was brief and he was gone.

Abby stood where she was, wondering at the abrupt ending to the evening. They'd enjoyed talking together. She'd felt some of her nervousness vanish and knew it was because she felt more comfortable around him.

And she had certainly expected a few more kisses at least before he left.

"So, what is it? You left abruptly to keep me off balance? Or because you're not really that committed to a relationship?'' she asked aloud. But the silence of her apartment was her only answer.

Promptly at seven the next evening the doorbell rang.

Opening the door, her heart caught. He looked so wonderful.

Without a word, he stepped into the apartment, closed the door and swept her into his arms.

His mouth found hers instantly, igniting flames of desire and passion. She encircled his neck, pressing against him to enjoy every speck of pleasure his touch brought.

In no time she was hot, breathing fast and caught up in his embrace. Doubts and insecurities fled. She could only feel, and revel in those feelings.

''You taste good enough to eat,'' he murmured against her jaw with nibbling kisses. Moving to her throat, he pressed his lips against the rapid pulse point. Moving back to her mouth, he kissed her deeply.

''Mmm, you're pretty tasty yourself, Doctor,'' she said when his lips trailed across her cheek.

The shrill ring of the phone startled them.

She leaned back and frowned.

''Expecting a call?''

She shook her head. ''The hospital would page me.''

It rang until the answering machine picked up. Elise's voice came through. ''Abigail, are you home? I need to find Greg and am hoping you—''

Abby swung around and hurried across the room to pick up the receiver.

''Hi Elise, Greg's right here. We were getting ready to go out. You just caught us.''

"Sorry, but this is important, can I speak with him?"

Abby handed him the receiver.

She watched as he listened, his face going hard.

"Then let him," he said. Listening again, he frowned.

She was dying to know what Elise was saying. Would Greg tell her? Or was family business not something discussed between lovers having an affair?

"Is she crazy? I can't talk to him! What would I say? It's none of my business."

He listened for quite a long time. "Okay, Elise, tell her I'll talk to him tomorrow. Not now, I'm on my way to dinner."

Abby waved her hand to get his attention. "We can postpone if you need to do something," she said softly.

"He can't do anything before Monday," Greg said into the receiver. "Okay. Okay, I'll see him tonight."

He hung up and looked at her. "Dave called Pam a little while ago—he wants a divorce. She's hysterical. Elise wants me to talk to him."

"Poor Pam. She really thought he'd come back," Abby said softly. "If you need to go, don't worry about me. We can have dinner anytime."

"We can have it now and I'll see him later."

"And have Pam worried all that time. If there is anything you can do or say to help, don't you think you should go?"

"I'm not going to be able to say anything to change the situation. They brought it on themselves."

"Still, she's your sister and Elise obviously feels you can help."

"No, she just wants me to do something."

''Because you're her big brother and she's always looked to you when things get tough.''

He nodded. Holding out his hand, he waited until Abby placed hers in it.

''Come with me, then. We'll visit Dave, then have our dinner.''

''Me? This is a family matter. I'm not family.''

''Doesn't matter. I want you, isn't that enough?''

Chapter Thirteen

Even meant a different way, the words *I want you* sent a thrill down her spine.

"I'll come if you think I can help."

"Hell, I don't think I can help. And it's sure not what I planned for this evening. Getting in the middle of a family fight is never wise."

"But Elise is counting on you. And Pam," she said gently.

"Looks that way, doesn't it? So are you coming with me?"

Abby hesitated a moment, then nodded. "Okay." It wasn't her idea of a great beginning to their evening, but she didn't want to desert Greg. How long could a stop at his brother-in-law's take?

A short time later they arrived at the inexpensive apartment building near the Western Addition. Greg parked the car in front and studied the building.

"With any luck, Dave won't be home."

Abby could only hope. Why had she agreed to come along? This had nothing to do with her. Greg would be better able to reason with his brother-in-law without a third party present.

"I'll wait in the car," she suggested.

"No, you don't. I want moral support."

Greg rang the bell. Behind the door, they could hear the soft murmur of a television.

Dave Schuler opened the door, looking first at Greg, then Abby, then back to Greg. An expression of resignation settled on his face.

"She sent her big brother to make everything all right again?" he asked sarcastically.

Pam's husband wasn't at all what Abby expected. He was tall and thin with receding hair. He looked as if he hadn't slept recently. For a moment she wondered what Pam saw in him. But it wasn't her place to judge.

"I can't make everything all right. Only you and Pam can do that. I wanted to talk to you, though," Greg said, stepping into the apartment.

"Sure, come on in." Dave stood aside.

"Dave, this is Abigail Trent, a friend of mine. Abby, Dave Schuler, Pam's husband."

"You know Pam?" Dave asked as he closed the door.

"We've met." She looked around. The apartment was neat but seemed neglected nonetheless. The television flickered, the noise filling the room. It seemed sad. And nothing like the homey place Pam lived. Where the two of them had lived together.

"You two are dressed up—is this an event?" Dave asked as he followed them into the living room. "Do you want to sit or can what you have to say be delivered standing up.''

"I'll stand," Greg said.

"Good, that means you'll be brief."

"I'll sit, if you don't mind," Abby said, hoping to defuse the tension with some semblance of normality. "We are on our way to dinner. Have you eaten?"

Dave shook his head. "I'll get something later."

"So did you find yourself?" Greg asked scathingly.

Dave met his gaze, his expression hardening. "None of your damned business."

"It is when it impacts my sister. What were you looking for that you couldn't find with her?"

"Maybe the same thing you were looking for when you dumped Michelle."

"I didn't dump Michelle, she chose her own road."

"Yeah, well I'm choosing mine now."

"Maybe you should have thought of that before you married Pam. Before the two of you had Bethany."

"Things aren't the same now as then. Maybe if I had known how it would be, I wouldn't have married her in the first place."

"Life is full of changes," Abby murmured.

Dave looked at her, as if surprised she'd spoken. "Full of changes, yeah, but there's change and then there's change."

"What does that mean?" Greg asked.

Dave shook his head and backed away. "What does it matter? You'll take Pam's side."

"Are there two sides?"

"Look, I married a nice girl who I thought would make us a home, have a bunch of kids and be there for me. Instead, we only had the one, and you know how complicated that birth ended up. Now she's off owning her own business, making tons of money with no time for her family or home. It's not the way I pictured it. And it's not what I want.''

Abby looked at Greg. ''Then the two of you should have a lot in common. That's not what Greg wants, either.''

''Huh?'' Dave looked at her again.

Abby stood. She didn't like feeling towered over by the two men who refused to sit.

''What is it with you men that you both think a woman's place is in the home and only the home? What if I told you from now on you had to stay home, no working outside the home at a paying job, just cleaning the house and taking your daughter to school and after-school activities. Would that be enough for you?''

''Don't be silly. I'm in business. I can't stay home.''

''It's not the same thing,'' Greg added.

''It is too the same thing. There are women who feel totally fulfilled staying home and caring for children and family. But what about those women who simply wish to work outside the home or whose children are grown, or so involved with their friends and school that they are rarely home? What of those women? Are all those women just to sort of fade into the background because it suits you to have them at your beck and call whenever you want them? What do they do the other twenty hours or so each day?''

''I never said a woman couldn't work,'' Greg said. ''I said marriage wasn't for me because a woman demands more than a doctor can give in time and commitment.''

''Yet you married Michelle,'' Dave said.

''A mistake. One I won't make again.''

"And you don't want to be married to Pam because she has her own business? Because she's not there for you whenever you want her to be?" Abby asked.

Dave stared at her, then his gaze dropped. "Her business means more to her than I do."

"Did she say so?" Greg asked.

"Does she say your business means more to you than she does when you have to work late?" Abby asked.

Dave shook his head. "That's different."

She rolled her eyes and glared at both men. "You two are from the Dark Ages. Neither of you has a glimmer of what a good, solid marriage is about. No wonder you can't make it work."

Both looked at her, Greg's gaze impassive, Dave's growing angry.

"You don't know anything about my marriage."

"Actually, Abby, you probably know less about marriage than either of us. Dave and I have been married, you never have."

If he had slapped her, he couldn't have surprised her more.

"I don't need to have firsthand experience to have a good idea that it takes work to keep a marriage solid. Work and compromise and dedication. Something Pam was willing to do, too bad you're not! But at least you have the chance. Some people never even get the chance to try!" She headed for the door.

"But since I know nothing about the institution, I'll wait for you in the car." She threw open the door and closed it behind her, resisting the childish urge to slam it.

She heard Greg call her name but didn't stop until she'd reached the sidewalk. Her feelings were suddenly aligned more with the unknown Michelle than Greg. Of all the chauvinistic comments to make. She was seething with anger. How dare he discount her comments—especially when he'd specifically asked her to come along!

Restlessly pacing by the car, she came up with several brilliantly scathing remarks she could have made. Why did she always think up the good stuff after the confrontation had passed?

Spotting a gas station at the far corner, she glanced back at the apartment. She would not enjoy dinner. In fact, she wasn't sure she was up to seeing Greg again anytime soon. She took a card from her wallet, scribbled a quick note and slipped it beneath the windshield.

In no time she'd walked to the gas station, called a cab and was heading for home.

Her first instincts were right. Greg Hastings was way out of her league. And she needed to remember that before she became more entangled with him.

Rubbing the ache in her chest absently, she feared it was already far too late. Maybe the break should come now. Forget the committee, ask to be relieved of her co-chair position and do her best to ignore the man in the future.

But even Abby, with her optimistic outlook, knew that would be far too easy. And so far nothing with Greg had been easy.

Abby paid the cab driver and turned.

''Hi, Abs.''

Startled, she looked up and saw Jeb Stuart.

''Jeb, what are you doing here?''

''I came to see you. Where've you been? You look—nice. Really nice.''

"Not a tart, huh?" she said, and started for the lobby door.

"Sorry, kid. But you have to admit you did go a bit over the top that night. What were you trying to do, lure every guy in sight?"

"No, I—" She couldn't tell him why she'd dressed so outrageously. In retrospect it had been foolish—both the doing and the reason. Jeb had been a friend, never anything more—except in her mind.

"Never mind. Want to come up?"

"I don't know. You look nice. Want to go someplace, have a drink or something?"

"I'd rather have dinner. I'm starving."

"We could go to that sushi bar we used to go with Carol."

For a moment the longing for the days when they'd been inseparable rose. Nothing stayed the same. Hadn't she just said that to Dave? Life went on. And good times could be found. Different, but still good.

"I'd like that, Jeb. I've missed you. What happened to Sara?"

He shrugged as he started walking toward his car. She fell into step.

"She only thought she wanted to date a doctor. She didn't like being stood up or being deserted if I got called in for emergency. Some women aren't meant to be doctors' wives."

As Abby slipped into the front seat of his small car, she wondered if he was right. He and Greg. Maybe there were women who weren't up to the rigors. But that didn't mean all women were.

"So are you swearing off women forever?" she teased.

He laughed softly. "I've missed you, Abs. You and

Carol. God, I still can't believe I'll never see her again.''

By the time he started the engine a few moments later, Abby had her own emotions under control.

"Have you heard from Mark?'' she asked, referring to Carol's fiancé.

"Yes. I talked with him last week. He's still half shell-shocked. Now there's a man who's swearing off women. Says he could never go through such a loss again.''

"They had their whole lives before them. And then—poof, it was gone.''

"All the more reason for us to live life to the fullest,'' Jeb said as he pulled out into traffic.

They'd always thought alike, she mused, feeling as if she'd come home again. Jeb was comfortable. Nothing like being with Greg. None of the sparks, the uncertainty, the exhilaration.

"I'm trying to do just that,'' she said firmly.

"So bring me up-to-date on what's been going on in your life,'' he invited.

It was late by the time Jeb delivered her home. Abby had enjoyed the evening more than she'd expected, except for the niggling guilt at walking out on Greg. That had been rude and uncalled-for—except she'd been so mad at him. Not that it excused her behavior. She knew she'd have to call and apologize. But not tonight.

The answering machine was blinking when she entered her apartment. Sighing, she passed by and headed for her room. She was not up to returning calls, nor listening to any messages she suspected Greg had left on the machine. Tomorrow, she'd listen to them—

The phone rang.

Holding her breath, she walked to the edge of the living room, listening when the answering machine picked up.

"Abigail, if you're there, pick up the damned phone!"

She could almost feel the anger radiating through the machine.

"I just want to know you're home safely, dammit. Pick up!"

She crossed over. "Hello, Greg, I'm home safely."

"Where the hell have you been? I've called every fifteen minutes since I discovered you'd taken off!"

"Sorry, I met a friend and we went to get a bite to eat. Then got to talking."

"We had a date," he said heavily.

"Well, that was before you so firmly put me in my place," she snapped.

"What are you talking about?"

"Shut up, Abigail, and don't offer any comments, because you don't have a clue about marriage and we don't want to hear anything you have to say," she said, the anger rising anew.

"That's not exactly what I said."

"That's exactly what you meant!"

There were a few seconds of silence, then he said, "I'm coming over."

"Please don't bother. I'm getting ready for bed and won't open the door. Good night." She hung up the phone and headed for the bedroom. When it rang a minute later, she ignored it.

So much for her great evening exploring new restaurants and spending time with Greg. If she had the evening to do over, she would not have gone with him. Or stayed in the car.

The next morning, Abby woke early and quickly dressed. She knocked on Kim's door to see if her friend wanted to go out for breakfast. Soon the two of them were at their favorite coffeehouse indulging in lattes and croissants. Abby refused to think about her breakfast at the bakery with Greg. It was as much fun to spend time with Kim!

The day was sunny and clear, with only a light breeze keeping the temperature moderate. When they finished, they decided to wander around downtown a bit, stopping in shops. Close to Pam's boutique, Abby was tempted to drop by, but thought better of it. What if Greg had taken his sister out for breakfast again? She didn't want to risk running into him.

"So, have you spent enough?" Kim asked, juggling the bags she carried. She frowned over at Abby. "How come you have only two and I have about eleven?"

"I exercised some prudence?" Abby asked, laughing. "I just bought a new wardrobe, remember? I don't need anything."

"What does need have to do with it?"

"Want me to carry any of those?"

"No, what I want is to find a place to sit down and have a hot fudge sundae, what do you say?"

"Sounds good to me." And it would keep her away from home that much longer. She knew she'd have a dozen messages when she returned.

Unless Greg had given up.

For some reason that worried her. Was she just playing hard-to-get? She didn't think she was the type to lead a man on.

"Okay, spill it," Kim said some time later when they were seated in an ice-cream parlor, orders already given.

"What?"

"Whatever makes you go into a trance at the weirdest times. Man trouble, I bet."

"Nothing I can't handle," Abby said stiffly.

Kim laughed. "Sure, but a problem shared is a problem halved. Tell."

Abby touched on the highlights, ending with her leaving Greg without going on to dinner the previous night. The very private and personal memories she kept to herself, but she knew Kim was bright enough to figure out what she'd omitted.

"So where do you want to go with this?" Kim asked as the sinfully rich sundaes were placed before them. "A wild fling or something more."

"There's no option. Greg is not in this for anything more than a wild fling."

"His loss. Get some experience, then move on to some guy who will at least be open to something more. Something lasting."

"Marriage," Abby said firmly. "I do want to get married. Maybe have a child or two. I'm afraid something will happen before I can do that—like with Carol."

"Not going to happen. That was fluky. Won't happen twice in your life."

"You don't *know* that."

"I can figure the odds. So enjoy yourself as long as you want. Can you do that knowing you have to walk away at the end?"

"I'll have to, won't I?" Abby said slowly. "I can

either break it off now—supposing he even wants to see me again—or later.''

"I'd go for later."

Suddenly Abby nodded, smiling. "Me, too. I thought I'd break it off after the charity ball for the hospital.''

"Play it by ear," Kim suggested, licking her spoon. "Love doesn't have a timetable."

Love? Abby wanted to deny she had any feelings of love. But she couldn't. Wasn't that what she had been trying to deny to herself? It wasn't possible— could she have fallen in love with Greg Hastings?

Well, that was sure one of the dumber things she'd ever done!

When Abby returned home, she put away her new purchases, wiped her palms on her jeans and headed for her phone. She owed Greg a call. Or a bunch, if the number of messages on her answering machine were any indication.

Ironically, she received his answering machine.

"Hi Greg, it's Abigail. I'm sorry about last night. I don't blame you if you never want to see me again. But if you do, give me a call." She hesitated, then added, "Otherwise, I guess I'll see you at the hospital.''

"Abby?" He broke into the recording. "Are you at home?"

"Yes."

"Do you want me to come over? Or do you want to come over here?"

"If you come here we can have stir fry or something for dinner," she suggested, almost holding her breath. He was not going to write her off without a chance to apologize at least. She'd have to be on her guard, giving nothing away. But at least they could salvage some of the weekend together.

"I'll be over about seven." He hung up before she could reply.

"In case I changed my mind?" she said softly. Despite the terms on which they parted, she felt a bubble of excitement at the thought of seeing him again.

Abby tried to remain calm when the doorbell rang at seven. She opened it and smiled brightly, hoping he couldn't see the rapid beat of her heart, or know how nervous she felt. He didn't look angry.

"Hi," she said.

"Hi yourself," he answered, pulling her into his arms and kissing her long and hard.

He ended the kiss and stared down into her eyes, his narrowed. "Let's get one thing clear—I did not say I didn't value your opinion. If the way I said you had no experience came out that way, I didn't mean it to. I wanted you there!"

"Okay."

"And if you run off on me again, I won't be held responsible for what I might do."

"Such as?"

"Camp out in your hallway?"

She smiled. "Elise practices that."

"You are too independent." He shut the door and motioned for her to precede him into the living room.

"Who did you go to dinner with last night? Kim?"

"No, she and I went out this morning for breakfast."

"I thought you were just ignoring my calls," he

said, sitting on the small love seat and patting the space beside him.

Daringly Abby risked sitting beside him. "How did you end up with Dave?" she asked.

"He and Pam were going to get together and talk today. When you walked out, he asked about your last comment. I told him about your friend Carol. It got him to thinking."

"So he should have. Sounded to me like a petulant spoiled boy wanting his own way."

Greg nodded. "He is. And I was, too. Your comments got me to thinking, too."

"Gee, I hope that wasn't too much of a strain," she murmured.

He nipped her arm. "Don't be sassy."

"So the ending will be happy?"

"I have no idea. But I called Elise and Pam both last night to tell them to leave me out of future negotiations. But by the time I called Pam, Dave had already arranged a date for them to meet today."

"And what did thinking do for you?" she asked.

"Made me glad I have the no-marriage rule. Think of the emotional price this breakup has cost not only Pam and Dave but their daughter, and families."

She shrugged, knowing it was futile to hope he'd change his mind just because she'd discovered she had fallen in love. But hope springs eternal.

"You still didn't tell me where you were last night," Greg said.

"I went to dinner with Jeb," she said recklessly. "He was here when I got home, and we began talking and decided to go to one of our favorite restaurants and eat together."

Greg didn't say anything and Abby dared a glance.

She could tell he was clenching his teeth. For a stunned moment she wondered if he was jealous?

But she quickly discounted that possibility. He'd have to have some feelings for her to feel jealous—even when there was no need.

"It was fun to see him again. You and he'd probably get on great."

"Why?"

"He seems to have developed the same ideas about doctors and wives as you. The only difference is he does see the possibility of another doctor understanding."

"Are you planning to see him again?" Greg asked carefully.

"I don't know. We were friends for years, but things change—just like Dave said. Want something to drink?" She jumped up before the conversation could turn in another direction. Needing distance, she hurried into the kitchen, and took down two wineglasses.

Greg followed her to the door and leaned against the jamb, watching her.

"Did you tell him about us?"

"What about us?"

"That we are seeing each other."

She shook her head, carefully pouring the wine. Taking one glass, she glanced at him, then placed it on the small table. Touching Greg at this moment wouldn't be a good idea. Especially when she wanted more than mere touching.

"I'll start supper."

Greg watched her, wondering what she was thinking. Did she have any idea the turmoil she'd caused with her casual comment about having dinner with Jeb Stuart. Especially when she'd originally planned to have dinner with *him* last night?

She looked beautiful even in the slacks and casual top. Maybe because of the way the slacks hugged her hips, her long legs.

The sweet floral scent she wore filled him as he breathed and he knew he'd forever associate it with Abby.

He was burning up for her, but clamped down on his basic needs. They could eat first, discuss other things besides Jeb and Dave and Pam.

But as soon as dinner was over, all bets were off.

Chapter Fourteen

"What else did you do today?" Greg asked as they sat at the table sometime later and began to eat. Abby had refilled their wineglasses.

"After Kim and I went to breakfast together, we went shopping. We had fun, and my pager was quiet all day."

"Do you normally get many calls?" he asked.

"A fair number. A pediatrician is more likely to have patients calling in the middle of the night and on weekends than a surgeon, I suppose. Kids get earaches at the strangest times."

"But you love it," he said as he watched her.

"Yes. I've wanted to be a doctor all my life. And it's all I hoped for."

"Even though we can't help everyone," he said, thinking about Mr. Jenkins's death. He still hated to lose, and that's what it always felt like when he lost a patient.

"I like knowing I'm doing the best I can. If I don't think I have the knowledge or experience needed, I'd call in help. But in most instances I can make a difference. Isn't that why you're a doctor?"

He nodded.

"Why did you become a surgeon? It's not the same as having a family practice. I'll see my patients periodically for years. You see yours for one operation and then they're gone. Don't you miss the contact, the building relationship?"

Greg shook his head. "It's not as if I don't meet them, I see them before and after the surgery. Beyond that, I like keeping my distance." He looked at her, wondering if she'd find fault in his reasoning. "It's easier not to build relationships."

She nodded. "Then you don't get hurt if someone dies. That's the hardest part, isn't it? I wondered all during med school if I'd be able to stand that. Another reason I chose pediatrics. More kids make it through than, say, geriatric patients. You must have gifted hands. I've heard a lot of great things about your practice—including what a high recovery rate you have."

Greg was uncomfortable with her praise. He did the job to the best of his ability, but never considered himself gifted.

She smiled saucily.

"And I have firsthand experience with the gifted-hands part, don't I?"

Greg felt the heat of arousal pool in his belly. He could see the color rise in her cheeks, and the defiant tilt to her head. She was unsure of herself, but out to show him she planned to be a full participant.

He wanted her. Glancing at the food still remaining, he pushed his plate away. One hunger had been assuaged. Another grew.

Standing, he stepped closer and was relieved when she caught her bottom lip between her teeth, but stood also, her eyes dancing.

"Not hungry anymore?" she asked softly, placing her hands on his shoulders.

"I told you, there are different kinds of hunger," he said, lowering his head for a kiss.

She tasted of spices and warm wine and Abigail. One touch and he ignited. It was unsettling how she affected him.

Knowing what awaited, he could be patient. His tongue traced her lips and then slid between to meet and mate with her tongue. The heady intoxication was immediate. He wanted more and he wanted it instantly. But years of discipline paid off and he took it slowly, stretching out each sensual moment.

They moved as if dancing, slowly around the table, kissing, nibbling, stroking, both of them prolonging the sensations that built and flamed. Moving along the short hallway, fingers fumbling with buttons, stroking bare skin, they headed for her bedroom as if they'd done it a million times before.

When they reached the darkened bedroom, Greg paused long enough to slip her shirt over her head.

Her lacy bra moved as she breathed and he remembered the sexy teddy she'd referred to. Would he ever get to see her in it? To take her out of it?

He watched her chest expand and contract, the soft skin creamy beneath the lace. He reached behind her to unfasten the garment and draw it deliberately down her arms. She shivered slightly, her nipples already tight and hard.

Flicking a quick glance into her eyes, he leaned forward and captured one rosy tip with his lips, unhurriedly drawing it into his mouth, feeling her gasp and her arms tighten around his neck. Her low moan of pleasure was stark in the silent evening. Her hands threaded themselves through his hair and held him against her.

Savoring the taste of her, the feel of her, the reaction to his touch, Greg drew the taut nipple deeper into the hot cavern of his mouth.

"Mmm, I had forgotten. How can anyone forget in only a few days?" Abby said, kissing his hair, moving to get closer.

Greg moved to unfasten her jeans. They were three steps from her bed, and he was about three seconds from exploding.

"Kick off your shoes and get the jeans off," he ordered, reaching for his own zipper.

Abby nodded, then slowly began to wiggle her way out of her jeans, making sure he watched every maneuver as she revealed inch after inch of skin.

"You're killing me," he whispered as she brushed against him while ostensibly trying to get out of the jeans.

She grinned. "Then we're even, because I think I'm dying of anticipation. Is it going to be as good as the other night?"

"You tell me," he said, blowing against her damp skin, watching as the nipple contracted.

Bare at last, she stepped closer and ran her hands over his muscles, over the slight covering of hair rasping against her palm. Flicking a nipple, she watched, fascinated while it tightened as hers had. Greg held on to his control by a thread. The novice had learned fast.

A slow smile crossed her face as she realized she could produce the same effect on him as he had on her. She darted a quick look up into his face, smiling even more at the look she discovered.

"Learning something new, are we, Dr. Trent?" he asked huskily, clenching his teeth to contain the groan of pleasure he longed to give way to. She was enchanting. He knew beyond a doubt she had no idea how she was driving him crazy.

Tilting her head, she nodded. "Mmm," she said in appreciation as she rubbed herself against him, bare skin to bare skin. The heat that was released would warm a building. "A doctor constantly has to continue her education."

In only seconds, Greg scooped her up to lay her on the big bed, and came down beside her. His mouth found hers and kissed her, then moved to taste every inch of her. His goal was to learn every hill, valley and secret place. To brand her with his touch and let her know in no uncertain terms how much he wanted her.

She squirmed and moved against him, about to shatter his resolve. But it was too soon. He wanted the night to last, for this to last. How he could postpone the driving need in his body seemed beyond him, but he wanted to try, to make this special for her. For them.

"Please, Greg," she whispered, rubbing against him, teasing him with the damp warmth he knew waited.

"Are you sure you're ready?" he murmured against her throat, his lips against her pulse point, feeling the rapid beat of her heart, feeling the heat that scorched her skin.

"Greg, I passed ready an hour ago." Her kisses were fiery, exquisite, inflaming.

She was so hot, he couldn't hold off another second.

He fumbled with the foil packet, tearing it open with his teeth.

Belying the urgent need for her, he slowly eased into the cradle of her thighs.

"Abby." His voice was tight with his need.

"What?" She opened her eyes to stare up at him.

"Watch me. I want to see you when I..."

He slid in. She was so tight he was afraid he'd hurt her, but the look in her eyes assured him it wasn't pain she was feeling. He'd never felt anything so wonderful. For a long moment they gazed at each other, the tension drawn so taut it felt about to snap. His hands went to her hips and held her as he withdrew slightly, then plunged in again.

"Oh." She bit her lip as she poised on the edge.

"Let it go. Let it go." He plunged in again. The next time he could feel her begin to go and gave it all he had.

Two seconds later shimmering waves of pure ecstasy poured through him. His body spun into the golden haze of rapture and Greg wondered if he'd ever be the same.

His climax was hard and hot and long. Pulsing into her he savored every millisecond, every inch of her, every sweet grabbing of her muscles, the scents that surrounded them. Her heat burned him, her body drained him, her essence enveloped him. Endless moments of delight, spinning heat and swirling sensations. Endless time with Abby.

Slowly reality returned. Slowly he became aware of her lying relaxed and quiet, tracing random patterns against his back. Balancing himself on his arms, he watched her. Her eyes were closed, her mouth tilted in a smile.

He couldn't resist kissing her, but the kiss was soft, tender—nothing like the passion-laced ones of earlier.

He was almost too tired to move. He relished the feel of her beneath him. Relished the heat between them that was only now fading.

What was it about Abby that was different from anyone else he'd ever known?

"You all right?" he said softly, brushing back her hair and threading his fingers through the soft tresses. If he'd thought about it, he might have predicted a few nights together would satisfy any needs he'd had. But each time only seemed to whet his appetite for more of her.

"Never better," she said with a beautiful smile.

"I know what you mean." He kissed her gently. He'd never felt like this before. It would take some getting used to. But it was something he wanted to get used to. For as long as she'd agree to their affair.

And if he handled things right, she'd be content for a long time.

Abby knew she was in trouble when she woke on Monday morning. Snuggled up against Greg's hard chest and long legs, she never wanted to move. And yet—nothing had changed.

Except for her entire life, she thought wryly. She'd never be the same, she mused, savoring the brush of his breath against her shoulder, the heat enveloping her. Why was she destined to fall for men who didn't want her?

Terry could be excused, even then she had at one time thought he was the love of her life. And Jeb was a friend, her stupid fantasies notwithstanding. Sooner or later she would have realized that. And friendship was valuable.

But with Greg she wondered if the feelings that consumed her would last forever. She hoped not. Surely she could meet someone in the next few months or years with whom she could fall in love, marry, share her life.

But would he have that air of cynical amusement, that lopsided smile, those killer brown eyes?

She forced the thoughts away. She didn't have time to dwell on them today. Time enough after the charity ball, when she made the break. For now, she'd take each day as it came and enjoy every moment. But in the end, she had to go for the long-term goal. And kiss her new love goodbye.

Slowly she shifted until she was on her back and could look at him. He was as sexy as ever with a trace of beard and his dark lashes like half-moons. She resisted the urge to trace her fingers over his jaw, to kiss him awake. He was sound asleep, obviously needing the rest.

She slipped from bed and headed for the bathroom. Keeping as quiet as she could, she was still surprised, after she was dressed, to discover Greg slept on.

Heading for the kitchen to prepare coffee, she thought she'd make omelettes for breakfast. Searching in the refrigerator to make sure she had a variety of ingredients, she wondered if she should wake him up, or let him sleep.

Did he have any appointments this morning? Could he afford to stay in bed as long as he wanted? For a moment she considered shedding her own clothes and rejoining him.

Letting her imagination soar, she pretended they were a couple, had made a commitment to each other and were spending a lazy day at home. What would constitute such a day for Greg? There was so much she didn't know about him. Did he like to read the paper, do the crossword puzzle? Or was he more inclined to go out to brunch somewhere and then do something more strenuous than lying around the house reading?

Glancing out the window at the beautiful spring morning, Abby suddenly longed to be a part of the day. Maybe she could take off early. They could squeeze in a jaunt to Fisherman's Wharf, ride the cable cars and visit tourist attractions.

Unless he had other plans, of course. It didn't pay to get too cocky, she thought.

"The coffee smells good," Greg said from the doorway.

She smiled and spun around. "Good morning."

Slowly he crossed the narrow kitchen and drew her into his arms. His kiss was all she remembered. Maybe she should forget her plans and just sweep him back to bed for the entire day.

"I think you wake me up better than coffee," he said a minute later, brushing her damp lips with his thumb.

Abby stepped away and busied herself getting him coffee. She'd almost said something stupid. It was hard to keep her emotions firmly under control. Yet she dared not say a word—not if she didn't want to scare him away before she was ready to call a halt to their affair.

"I need to get home to change. And I want to call Pam and see if she and Dave reached any verdict," he said, sipping the hot brew, then placing his cup on the counter.

"Call from here," Abby suggested.

He hesitated a moment, then shook his head. "I'll call from home."

His kiss distracted her for a moment, but the bottom line was, she realized after he left, he hadn't wanted to involve her any more in his family problems.

How often did she need to be hit over the head with the fact he was not in the relationship for the long haul?

She was only making matters worse by delaying the inevitable. Why wait until after the ball? If she asked another man to escort her, she could tell Greg it was over now.

"I don't want to go with anyone else," she said aloud. She'd stick to her original plan—go to the ball and then end their personal relationship. She'd learn to deal with seeing him at the hospital. If it became too painful, she could always look for a different location.

It was hard to keep her mind on the day at hand and not fantasize about a future, but Abby managed. It helped that her caseload was pretty heavy, and she had two more new patients with chicken pox to squeeze in. Mondays were always hectic.

She knew Greg had a major surgery in the morning, and didn't expect to see him that day. But by the time she was ready for bed, she was annoyed he hadn't even called. She knew she could call, but didn't. Was she trying to prove something?

Tuesday afternoon she was writing notes for files when Mike knocked on the opened door.

"Got a minute, Abigail?" he asked, walking in.

"Sure." She tossed down the pen. "What's up?"

"Nothing much, more's the pity. I'm trying to get a particularly elusive young woman to go to the hospital charity event with me. No luck, so far, so I came to see if you could offer any suggestions."

"And this elusive young woman would be?"

"Elise Hastings, of course." He sat on the edge of her desk and fiddled with the pen she'd just put down.

"You asked and she said no? Is she going with someone else?"

"No. She doesn't plan to go at all. It's not her goal in life to support every fund-raiser the hospital has just because her brother works here."

Abby laughed. "That sounds just like Elise." She studied Mike for a moment, her smile fading. "You really like her, huh?"

He met her gaze and nodded morosely. "For all the good it does me. I've never met a more cynical person, or one who refuses to even give dating a chance."

"Then I'm not sure I can help."

"You know her, talk to her for me, please? Sometimes I don't think it's me so much as she just doesn't have a high regard for men in general. And if that's the case, maybe I can change her mind. But if it's just me…"

"I don't think I can do anything, but I don't mind asking her why she keeps saying no. Just how serious are you?"

"It's early to tell, but I think I'm as serious as it

comes. We've talked on the phone a lot. She'll go that far. But the moment I press to get together in person, she erects barriers ten feet high. When you canceled the other night, I tried to get her to go out with me. No dice.''

''I think the entire family is gun-shy about relationships.''

''I'm not asking for forever, I just want a date to the hospital ball!'' he said, leaning forward for emphasis.

''Abigail is already booked,'' Greg said from the doorway. He gave Mike a hard look. ''Didn't she tell you?''

Mike slid off the desk and smiled down at Abby. ''Actually, she didn't. You taking her?''

Greg nodded once.

''Lucky Abigail,'' Mike said, slipping his hands into his trouser pockets. He didn't move from beside the desk.

Abby jumped up and stepped to the opposite side of her desk, eyeing the two men as they stared at each other. She swore she could feel the tension rise.

''I didn't tell him, because he didn't ask,'' she said, rounding the corner of the desk.

''Sounded to me like he was asking,'' Greg said.

''He was asking for Elise.''

''Elise?'' Greg looked at her, puzzled. ''My sister, Elise?''

Abby nodded, crossing her arms over her chest.

''I didn't know you knew her,'' Greg said to Mike.

''We've talked on the phone a few times. She's hardheaded and stubborn, but I still want to take her to the dance.''

''I said I'd talk to her,'' Abby said.

"Why? She's made her position clear. Obviously she doesn't want to go. Or at least not with Mike."

"So that's it. Let it go because she said no?" Mike asked. He stepped forward. "I don't give up so easily. Thanks, Abigail. I'll talk to you later." He walked past Greg.

Greg ignored Mike and watched Abby. "I thought when I heard him, he was inviting you."

She stood where she was, hearing the echo of his words *she's made her position clear.* So had Greg—why was she ignoring it?

"So you said." Had that been a flash of jealousy she'd spotted? Highly unlikely. "Can I do something for you? I have another patient in a few minutes."

He shook his head. "It's not important. Just stopped by to say hi. I'll pick you up Saturday at seven."

"We don't have to be there early to make sure everything is going the way we want?"

"We'll still arrive early enough to insure that. But the staff at the hotel is trained for such events. Nothing will go wrong."

The conference was due to start Thursday morning, continue through midafternoon Saturday, and end with the charity ball. Despite her trepidation when first assigned to the committee, the actual work had been minimal. Most of it had been finished before her assignment. And Rose had made sure everything ran like clockwork.

"Fine, I'll see you then." With a pang she realized he had said nothing about the intervening days. Of course, they would both be busy once the conference began.

Greg nodded and leaned forward enough to touch his lips to hers. "Sounds like a brush-off to me. So

I'll just have to make do with that until Saturday,'' he said, his eyes dancing in familiar, cynical amusement.

"I know you'll be busy between now and then—"

"But not after the ball."

"No, not after the ball." By then she'd have said her piece and ended their brief affair. It had been glorious. But even naive doctors knew all good things came to an end.

Chapter Fifteen

Dressing for the ball Saturday evening, Abby reviewed the conference. She'd been introduced to dozens of the most preeminent physicians in their field. She'd learned more through the workshops than she'd expected, and had handled the minor problems that cropped up with a flair for organization that surprised her.

She was still basking in the praise Dr. Taylor had given that afternoon. All in all, the committee appointment had worked far better than she had anticipated.

And tonight was for pure pleasure. Rose had reassured her that afternoon that she'd double-checked every aspect of the charity event. The donations and tickets had brought in well in excess of projections. The hotel was ready to receive their guests, and there were no problems expected. From the forceful way

Rose said it, Abby knew it probably would run perfectly.

She donned a pale soft blue gown with low-cut bodice, long skirt and wispy sleeves. It was brand-new, and she couldn't wait for Greg to see it. She was still focused on her plan to end their relationship after tonight. If she was ever to meet the man of her dreams and marry, she needed to cut her ties with the man who had sworn off marriage.

Remembering Carol, she tilted her chin. It would be hard—and for the next few months she'd probably regret her decision a dozen times. But she had her entire life ahead of her, and she had to make the most of it. Her goals and Greg's were different. He'd shown her a lot over the past few weeks, given her an idea of how she wanted her marriage to be, of the feelings she wanted for her mate. Time she put her knowledge into play.

She studied her reflection in the mirror, intrigued to see how blue her eyes looked, how flushed with color her cheeks were. Her hair curled and cascaded across her shoulders, bright and shining with the highlights. She felt sophisticated and confident. There was nothing anyone could fault this evening.

When the doorbell rang, she was ready. Opening the door, she smiled when she saw him. The poignancy of it being the last time caused her heart to catch. Then it resumed its rapid beat—normal whenever Greg Hastings was around.

"You look beautiful," he said, letting his gaze roam over her.

"Thank you. I think you look super in a tux. Maybe we should change the dress code at Merrimac."

He shook his head. "Once in a while is fine, but I prefer more comfort on a daily basis. Ready?"

She nodded, reaching for her wrap.

As they stood side by side in the elevator, Abby realized he hadn't kissed her. Was it to make sure he didn't muss her makeup? Or was he also having thoughts about bringing their brief fling to an end?

When they were in the car heading toward Union Square, Greg flicked her a glance.

"Pam and Dave will be here tonight."

"They are seeing each other again?" Abby asked.

"Yes. Taking things slowly, and they started seeing a marriage counselor. But each loves the other. They think they just need help in adjusting to the changes in their lives. Bethany will be thirteen soon, and before they know it, out on her own. Not only do they need to deal with the changes in their lives now, but the inevitable ones to come."

"I'm glad. I wish more people took time to give marriage their all. So many seem quick to get a divorce if things aren't going their way."

"Such as Michelle and me?"

Abby shook her head. "I think your circumstances were different. There's no excuse for infidelity."

"Not something you'd do," Greg murmured.

"I'd make very sure of my feelings before entering into marriage. Then I'd do my best to keep it a strong relationship. No, cheating is not something I'd ever do."

They pulled in front of the hotel and turned the car over to valet parking. Entering the ballroom a few moments later, Abby paused for a moment to enjoy the elegance before her.

The chandeliers sparkled overhead, the lighting subdued yet plentiful, casting a flattering glow on everyone. The orchestra was already playing when they entered, and a dozen or so couples were dancing. Abby noticed none of the other men looked as distinguished as Greg. She stepped closer, sliding her hand around his arm, glad he was her escort.

Procuring a glass of wine for each of them from a passing waiter, he nodded toward a row of tables. "Want to find a place?"

"Sure." She wound her way through to a vacant one on the edge of the dance floor. He placed the drinks on the table and held the chair for her.

"Unless you'd rather dance first," he asked, leaning closer, his breath brushing against her cheek.

She nodded.

He took her in his arms and moved them onto the dance floor.

Abby gave a soft sigh and relaxed, delighted beyond belief to be in his arms again. Tingles radiated from his hand up her arm. When his right hand pressed her tightly against him, she almost missed a step, then recovered, reveling in the feel of him, the strength of his long muscular thighs as they brushed against hers, the hot potency of his hand on her back, holding her so closely she couldn't move away. Not that she wanted to.

She longed to turn her face up to his, wanted him to kiss her again. She wished they weren't in a ballroom full of people. Or that she'd instituted one at her apartment. Was there any hidden meaning in no kiss?

She recognized some of the doctors from the hospital, waving and nodding to friends and acquaintances. The ballroom was getting more crowded as more and more couples arrived. It was a magical time.

She snuggled closer and looked up to meet the dark glitter of his eyes as he bore down into hers.

He didn't say a word, but his breath fanned gently across her cheeks and she could not move for anything. Her gaze locked with his and Abby feared she was lost.

Slowly her hand crept up to thread her fingers into the thick hair at the back of his skull. Gently she tangled her fingers, moving seductively against him, wishing she were brave enough to pull him down to kiss her, knowing she was not. Not with so many people around. She'd have to bide her time.

"You learn fast, Abby," he said softly. They were touching from chest to knees, and Abby wondered breathlessly how much longer her legs would support her. She was tingling all over and wanted him to kiss her so badly she actually ached.

Running her tongue across her dry lips brought a groan from Greg as he followed its path and gave a lingering look at the dampness she left behind.

When the music stopped, he released her, catching her hand and threading his fingers through hers. He turned to survey the crowd. Speaking easily to one or two other couples, Greg introduced her to doctors and their wives she didn't know as they made their way back to the table.

"This should bring in a lot of money for the hospital," she said, striving for conversation, anything to take her mind off her body's yearning. Maybe it had been a mistake to come with him. Could she break it off tonight?

"It looks like it. The conference went well, too. Ben is already talking about another one in a couple of years. Want to be on that committee?"

She smiled. "We'll see."

Where would she be in two years? She couldn't even venture a guess. Would she be married by then? Have a baby?

The music changed and the tempo picked up.

"Ready for another dance?" Greg asked.

She nodded and stood—surprised when he reached for her hand and spun her around so fast her hair swept out and her skirt swung around, entangling both their legs. She leaned back against his strong arm and laughed, her eyes sparkling in delight.

"Fancy stepwork, Doctor."

"It could stand some improvement," he muttered wickedly and proceeded to dance across the floor with her, swaying and turning and showing her that a placid pace wasn't the only kind of dancing he could do.

Abby loved it. As they tried new steps, she'd move as he directed, closer, farther, always to be drawn back against him again and again in a teasing erotic dance of awareness. Her body was singing. When she realized his foreplay, she began to match him in each audacious move. Her eyes sparkled as she gazed flirtatiously into his. The smile she couldn't hide held a hint of mystery, a teasing promise of future delights.

Her breasts brushed against his chest, titillating, tantalizing, but never remaining long. She exaggerated the dips, loving the strength of his arms holding her. Swinging her hips, she knew she was being deliberately provocative, but seeing the fire in his eyes inspired her and she pushed it to the limit.

"They will have us out of here in no time if you keep that up," he muttered, drawing her tightly against him, molding her body the length of his as his hand splayed across her back.

"You inspire me," she said back, moving her hips beneath his hand, delighting in the soft sound that he made deep in his throat. Abby was heady with a feeling of power and desire. She loved Greg Hastings, and even though she knew she was playing with fire, she didn't care. This was her night and she was going to enjoy it to the fullest.

They were both breathing hard when the song ended. Staring at each other over the slight distance that separated them, Abby longed to throw herself into his arms and beg him to love her.

"Quite the display. Didn't know you were so accomplished, brother dear."

Greg and Abby swung around to see Elise smiling sassily at both of them. Beside her, dressed in a midnight tux, was Mike Adams. His sly, teasing smile encompassed the two and he nodded at Abby.

"Mike, how nice to see you." Abby spoke first. "And with Elise?"

He nodded. "Thanks to you?" he asked.

Abby shook her head, but Elise contradicted her.

"Of course thanks to Abby. If not for her, I would never have come. I'm still reserving my opinion on whether it was a smart move or not."

"Definitely one smart move," Mike said.

"Nice of you to come, Elise," Greg said.

"Especially when he first thought I wanted to come with Abigail," Mike said audaciously, laughing a little.

"Exactly what I meant."

"So after that display, what else can we expect from you and Abby?" Elise said. "I thought you were going to introduce her to some more eligible men."

"Go stir up trouble elsewhere, Elise. I have enough

without you adding to it,'' Greg said, glancing at Abby.

She just smiled at him, but for a moment she wondered if he suspected.

''Mom did a great job, don't you think?'' Elise turned to survey the ballroom.

''Was your mother involved with this?'' Abby asked.

''Involved? She's the chairman of the committee that put this together. And it's only one of many she does each year.''

''I told you my mother worked at charitable events,'' Greg said.

''Worked at—yes, ran them—no.'' Abby looked at Elise. ''Has she always been so involved in the hospital?''

''It's just one of her charities. She does a lot for the opera and the AIDS clinics as well. I've often thought, if she'd tried, she could have been the CEO of some major corporation.''

''But she didn't need to work,'' Greg inserted.

''Might as well have gotten paid for all the work she's done over the years,'' Elise said.

''I thought she stayed at home and took care of all of you,'' Abby said, glancing between brother and sister.

Elise shrugged. ''She was home a lot, but always on the phone with one committee member or another. Mostly I remember how many nights she was gone to committee meetings. Or the events themselves. She has a high energy level and is involved in lots of projects. Everyone knows if you want a successful event, get Susan Hastings.''

Abby stared at Greg. He glanced down at her, puzzled at her expression.

The music started. Before Greg could ask Abby, however, she received a tap on her shoulder.

"A dance, my dear?" Dr. Taylor was smiling at her.

Smiling politely, Abby nodded. "I'd be delighted."

The older doctor swiftly moved them out on the dance floor, smiling urbanely and making innocuous small talk with her. She tried to be polite, but she was dying to think about what Elise had just said. Obviously Greg's mother wasn't the paragon stay-at-home mother he wanted for a wife. Was his idea a rebellion against his mother's role? Or did he remember her being home differently from what Elise remembered? Had she become involved in charitable works after her children were grown?

That wasn't what Elise had said.

When Dr. Taylor began to discuss the conference, Abby knew she needed to pay attention. How long could a song last?

When the orchestra ended the song, Abby stepped back, glad to be released. She scanned the crowd, looking for Greg.

"Care to join us for a few moments?" the doctor invited. "Dr. Emory was asking about you at dinner. He'd like to see you once more before flying home."

"I should find Dr. Hastings."

He glanced around the ballroom, then shook his head. "I don't see him anywhere. Come and have a drink with us and I'll take you around afterward and we'll find him."

Greg watched Abby dance away with Dr. Taylor. He couldn't very well deny every other man present a chance to dance with her, much as he wanted to. But he didn't like the idea of her dancing with anyone else, even a man old enough to be her father. He watched her as long as he could. Once the crowd came between them, he turned back to discover his sister and her date had also joined the dancers on the floor.

Walking back to their table, he sat down to wait out the song. When it ended, he'd find Abby and take her home. He liked dancing with her, but he liked her naked in his bed even better.

When she arrived at the table twenty minutes later, he was getting angry.

"Nice of you to remember who you came with," he said as she joined him.

"Sorry, but Dr. Taylor wanted me to speak to some of the people who attended the conference. I can't believe how many people are here. How many were they expecting?"

"I have no idea."

"Hi, Abby. Care to dance?" Jeb Stuart stopped at their table.

"Hi, Jeb. Sure." She smiled at her old friend and rose.

Greg rose as well. "I believe this dance is mine," he said.

"Oh?" Abby looked at him. "Okay. Sorry, Jeb. Maybe another one?"

"I'll be around," he said easily.

"Until the next sexy blonde comes along," Greg said as he swung Abby into his arms and they began moving to the slow show tune.

"He's a friend, you know that."

"Not a very good one if he cuts you out for some blond bimbo."

"He's been a fine friend. It's not his fault I imagined myself feeling more for him than he felt for me."

Greg looked into her eyes. "So you imagined that, huh?"

She nodded, moving her gaze.

"So what do you imagine you feel for me?" Greg asked.

Her eyes locked with his. "Friendship."

"That's all?"

She hesitated, then slowly nodded. "Isn't that what you wanted? Friendship?"

"Yes. Glad you didn't get it confused. So many women imagine themselves in love without any reason."

"No, we wouldn't want anyone to imagine themselves in love without any reason. There's no such thing, is there, Greg?"

"Not that I can see."

"Carol and Mark were in love," Abby said slowly. "And planning a future together. You know I want that, too."

"So you've said."

"I think I need to get on with finding someone who wants the same things I do."

Greg spun her around and tightened his grip on her hand. "Which means?"

"I think I should ask for those introductions you've promised me. It's time."

"And our affair?"

"Dr. Hastings?" A waiter tapped him on the shoulder at the same time his beeper sounded.

"Yes." Greg released Abby.

"Sorry, sir, a call from your hospital." The man held out a portable phone.

Greg took it, wishing a moment later he had not, though the beeper number was also the hospital. There'd been a multiple car pileup on the Bay Shore Freeway. All available surgeons were being asked to assist. Damn. He cut the connection and walked off the dance floor.

"Trouble?" Abby asked.

"Emergency at the hospital." He noticed another surgeon leaving quickly. "I have to go."

"Do you need me to go, too?"

"No. I'm sure they'll call you if they need a pediatrician. I don't know how long I'll be."

"That's all right. I'll see myself home." Some of the disappointment she felt showed in her eyes, but she pasted a smile on anyway. She wished they had finished the discussion. She didn't want to have to go through it again.

But he didn't need any recriminations if he was needed.

"That way you won't have to worry about me or try to return."

"Very well. I'll call you." With a curt nod, Greg turned and walked away.

Abby watched, unable to believe her evening was over. Three dances was all they'd had.

Jeb claimed her for a dance. Then Mike took a turn, he and Elise urging Abby to join them. But there was no reason to remain. Excusing herself from Mike and Elise a short time later, she gathered her wrap to leave.

Prevailing upon the doorman to call her a cab, she sank against the back seat as the door shut behind her. She closed her eyes in disappointment. It wasn't how she had expected the evening to end.

Abby didn't know what happened next, but the cab spun wildly. The sound of squealing brakes and screeching metal filled the air. She opened her eyes just as a huge truck filled her sight, its lights filling the interior, bearing down on them as if the truck would crush the cab. For an instant she remembered Carol, then everything went black.

Chapter Sixteen

"Dr. Hastings." The nurse stepped into the surgery, staying well away from the patient.

"Yes?"

"Are you almost finished here?"

He looked up. "Another one waiting?" he asked. He thought this was the last. "I'm closing now."

"It's Dr. Trent. She's in the emergency room. She was involved in a car accident tonight—"

"What?" For a second a searing pain cut through him. He looked at the body on the table and saw nothing. Abby in a car accident? Like her friend Carol?

Damn! She'd talked about being scared she'd end up like her friend. It hadn't been a premonition, had it?

He glanced at the senior resident assisting. "Close for me," he ordered, stepping back. He crossed the operating room to join the nurse. "What happened? How is she?"

"I don't know the details, only that she is down in ER and they sent word up here."

He pulled off his gloves and cap, tossing them into the hazardous waste bin, never slowing his pace. His heart began to beat with fear. Abby had to be all right. She couldn't have been killed like her friend. She had her whole life ahead of her.

And she wanted to get married, have a family, practice medicine.

As had Carol.

He punched the button for the elevator. Impatiently waiting a couple of seconds, he couldn't stand the delay. He almost ran for the stairs, did run down them.

Pushing into the emergency room a few moments later, he looked around. It was still a zoo, patients backed up due to the pileup on the freeway. He strode down the hall, glancing at each person on a gurney, sidestepping around harried nurses.

Pausing at the desk, he caught the senior nurse's eye.

"Dr. Trent was brought in, I understand."

She nodded. "Number seven."

He spun around and headed for cubicle seven. Taking a breath before pushing aside the curtain, he stepped inside.

Abby was lying on the examination table, her eyes closed. There was a small row of sutures near her hairline, a dark bruise surrounding it. It was the only color. She looked as pale as...

"Abby?" he said softly, stepping up to the table.

She opened her eyes, tried to smile.

"Kim was wrong. She said the chances of the same thing happening were too great to even worry about."

He had to touch her. His fingers brushed her hair. It was matted with blood.

"She was right, you're alive."

"Umm."

He reached for her chart just as a young intern entered.

Greg ignored him, quickly scanning the chart.

"Did someone call you, Dr. Hastings?" the young man asked. "I don't think she needs any surgery. Do you have internal pain you didn't tell me about?" he asked Abby, suddenly looking worried.

She shook her head.

"I'm taking her home," Greg said. "As soon as you release her."

"Your surgery?" Abby asked.

"Finished. And they can find someone else if they need anyone. You're more important."

She blinked, as if unable to understand plain English.

"She can go, but someone needs to watch her. She has a slight concussion. She's bruised, wrenched her knee, and we sutured the cut. Don't wash the hair until tomorrow and don't pull on the sutures."

"I know the drill," Greg said, his eyes only for Abby. Even now the relief wasn't as heartfelt as he wanted. *She could have been killed.* Fear rose.

"What happened?"

"I had on my seat belt," she said.

Greg looked at the other doctor.

"Truck's brakes failed, plowed right into a cab. The driver was badly hurt. He was already sent up to surgery. I don't know his condition. She's okay. Or will be in a few weeks. She was lucky, wearing the seat belt saved her from more serious injury.''

"Carol wasn't wearing hers," Abby said, trying to sit up.

Greg helped her up until she swung her legs over the side, wincing when she bent her right knee.

"Pain meds." The young intern handed a packet to Greg. "She should be checked out again tomorrow." He nodded and left.

Greg lowered his mouth and brushed a quick kiss across her lips. "I was terrified when the nurse came into OR. She didn't know anything, only that you'd been in a car crash. All I could think about was your friend."

"Me, too. It happened so fast. I was afraid history was repeating itself and I'd miss out on everything like Carol. Can you take me home?"

It seemed to take an eternity but finally the nurses brought a wheelchair, fitted her with a set of crutches and pronounced her ready to leave. Greg had gone to change, then brought his car around and assisted her to the front seat. Settling her in, he fastened her seat belt.

"I'm not an invalid," she protested.

"Just be glad it wasn't worse."

"I am." She watched him climb in the driver side and pull away from the hospital. In only minutes he pulled into his apartment complex.

"I want to go home," she said.

"Not a chance."

Despite her protests, he carried her up to his apartment, setting her on her feet at the door while he unlocked it.

"That was the worst few minutes of my life," Greg said as soon as he shut the door behind them.

She turned and stared up at him, balancing on one foot. She shook her head, wincing at the throbbing. Was she hearing him correctly? Had her mind snapped or were the pain pills causing her to imagine the words to ease the pain in her heart?

He stepped forward and gathered her into his arms, carrying her to the sofa and placing her on it as delicately as if she were spun glass.

His mouth dropped to hers and his lips teased hers open before he swept her into a kiss straight from heaven.

Then he pulled back a scant few inches and gazed down at her, his eyes searching every inch of her face, as if memorizing it.

"Are you really all right?"

She nodded, then closed her eyes. "I will be. I was lucky, wasn't I? But it's scary how close to death I came."

She opened her eyes and touched his cheek, smiling sadly.

"I love you, Greg. I think I have for weeks. But all along I've wanted more than you can give me. I want a husband and a family. I guess I'm old-fashioned that way. I want more than a wild fling with a sexy doctor."

"I know."

"I need to get on with my life," she said slowly. "I need to live every second to the fullest. I knew that from what happened to Carol. Tonight just emphasized it."

"Marry me, Abigail Trent. Let me be your husband. Let me be the one you have babies with."

She stared at him.

"What?"

He looked into her eyes, hiding nothing. "Don't tell me this is so sudden. What do you think we've had over these past few weeks?"

"A wild, wonderful affair. You taught me a lot, starting with kisses and moving on to the most wonderful experiences of my life," she answered promptly.

"It was wonderful. But I was being taught, too. And what we have, it's not like anything else. You are not like anyone else. But the clincher came tonight."

"Tonight?"

"When I heard you had been in a car crash, all I could do was remember your friend, and the tragic early end to her life and dreams. Those few minutes between hearing about the accident and seeing that you were going to be all right were the worst I've ever had. I never want to go through something like that again!

"But it showed me what I kept trying to deny. I love you, Abby. I don't know since when, but I knew for certain tonight when I thought you were seriously injured, or even dead."

"You love me? I thought you didn't believe in love."

"Even smart surgeons can learn a thing or two. Or maybe it was that I've never been in love before. What I feel for you is different from what I felt for Michelle. Deeper, more encompassing. I can't explain, except that with you I feel whole and without you I feel like a shell."

"You truly love me?"

"I truly love you. Will you marry me?"

Her eyes filled with tears, but the radiance of her smile convinced him she was not a bit unhappy as she nodded her head.

He kept the kiss gentle, though he wanted to shout to the world. She was going to marry him!

Endless moments spun on a cloud of love and rapture, Abby never wanted it to end. Her heart beat in its frantic tempo, his mouth wreaked delight with his featherlight caress. *He loved her!* She didn't have to break off seeing him tonight. Greg wanted to marry her! She would get to see him every day of her life from now on.

Her hands clutched his pleated dress shirt, her fingers rubbed against the hot skin beneath the buttons. She wanted him so much.

"I thought you wanted a stay-at-home wife," she said.

"I did. But I want you more."

"Did your mother really work as hard as your sister said?" Abby asked.

"Yes."

"Yet you felt loved, cherished."

"Of course."

"But if what Elise said was true, your mother wasn't home any more than I will be. I can be just as good a wife, just as loving a mother. It's not the hours you spend being a wife and mother, it's what you give to the hours. I love you, Greg. You'd always come first in my life. But my profession is important to me, too. I need it."

He leaned back, tilting her chin with a finger. "I would never ask you to give up your work, any more than you'd ask me. We'll do what Pam and Dave are doing, learn ways to compromise and accommodate all the changes in our lives. But we'll build our marriage so strong, nothing will prevail against it!''

''That's the most important part, isn't it, the commitment?''

''Yes. Now that I think about it, there were a lot of days when my mother was gone from sunup to long past sundown. We had someone else do most of the cooking. You and I can do that if we need to. Funny, I only remember the fun times my family's shared over the years. And the fact my mother was always there when I needed her.''

''So we'll make good memories, too. And I'll be there for you and any children we might have.''

''I love you, Abby. You once asked me if Michelle was the love of my life. She wasn't. You are, just as you are. And part of what makes you what you are is being a doctor. Make room for me in your life and I'll make sure you never regret it.''

''Medicine is just one facet of me. I think now that without you I would feel so lost, so alone, so incomplete. I love you, Greg, forever.''

''That might be long enough.''

She beamed up at him, one finger tracing his lips as her eyes shone. Her face was bruised, her hair a tangled, matted mess. A bandage covered the line of sutures. All makeup had been washed off.

''You look beautiful, sweetheart,'' Greg said, kissing her again.

''Of course you realize I'm primarily taking this drastic step because of one thing,'' he said a few minutes later, holding her firmly in the circle of his arms.

''What?'' She looked at him with uncertainty until

she saw the teasing light in his eyes. Relaxing against him, she smiled again, waiting breathlessly for his next words.

"To see you in that indecent teddy you sleep in."

Abby blushed. "I lied," she whispered, her eyes bright with love. "My gown is virginal, white, and very modest. Just as you guessed."

He shouted with laughter, hugging her tightly against him.

"Then that will be my wedding present to you, my love. Wearing it on our wedding night will be yours to me," he said in the low, sexy, honeyed voice she loved. He sealed that bargain with what had started all their love—a kiss.

* * * * *

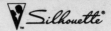

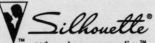

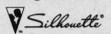

Silhouette —

where love comes alive—online...

eHARLEQUIN.com

shop eHarlequin

- ♥ Find all the new Silhouette releases at everyday great discounts.

- ♥ Try before you buy! Read an excerpt from the latest Silhouette novels.

- ♥ Write an online review and share your thoughts with others.

reading room

- ♥ Read our Internet exclusive daily and weekly online serials, or vote in our interactive novel.

- ♥ Talk to other readers about your favorite novels in our Reading Groups.

- ♥ Take our Choose-a-Book quiz to find the series that matches you!

authors' alcove

- ♥ Find out interesting tidbits and details about your favorite authors' lives, interests and writing habits.

- ♥ Ever dreamed of being an author? Enter our Writing Round Robin. The Winning Chapter will be published online! Or review our writing guidelines for submitting your novel.

Don't miss the reprisal of
Silhouette Romance's popular miniseries

When
King Michael of
Edenbourg goes
missing,

his devoted
family and loyal
subjects make it
their mission to bring
him home safely!

Their search begins March 2001 and continues through June 2001.

On sale March 2001: **THE EXPECTANT PRINCESS**
by bestselling author **Stella Bagwell** (SR #1504)

On sale April 2001: **THE BLACKSHEEP PRINCE'S BRIDE**
by rising star **Martha Shields** (SR #1510)

On sale May 2001: **CODE NAME: PRINCE**
by popular author **Valerie Parv** (SR #1516)

On sale June 2001: **AN OFFICER AND A PRINCESS**
by award-winning author **Carla Cassidy** (SR #1522)

Available at your favorite retail outlet.

Silhouette®

Where love comes alive™